Coast
to
Coast

www.cyberworldpublishing.com

This book is copyright © Olivia Stowe 2011
First published by Cyberworld Publishing in 2011.
Cover design by S Bush © 2011
Cover photos - Hollywood Sign © Byron
Moore | Dreamstime.com
Roulette Table © Yuri Bershadsky | Dreamstime.com
Ebook ISBN 978-1-921879-34-0
Print ISBN 978-1-921879-35-7

All characters in this book are the product of the author's
imagination and no resemblance to real people, or implication of
events occurring in actual places, is intended.

Published by Cyberworld Publishin
Jindalee St, Toronto, NSW
Australia

Books By Olivia Stowe

Charlotte Diamond Mysteries
By the Howling
Retired With Prejudice
Coast to Coast

Other books
Fiddler's Rest
Spirit of Christmas
Chatham Square

Coast

to

Coast

Olivia Stowe

Chapter One

Charlotte Diamond felt completely out of her element in the Hollywood arena. If her good friend and companion, Brenda Boynton—who she had to refer to as Brenda Brandon in this environment—didn't sympathize so well and wasn't throwing her a lifeline constantly, Charlotte would have caught the next plane back to Baltimore.

She wasn't used to being out of her element. Until recently she'd been the chief investigator for the Maryland office of the FBI in Annapolis and she had commanded any room she entered—in presence as well as stature. She did not mind being in Brenda's shadow, either in Hollywood or in the riverside retirement village of Hopewell on the Choptank back on an inlet into the Chesapeake Bay in Maryland where the two women had met and melded so well. But Charlotte felt huge and ugly and so inconsequential in the environment the box office movie actress Brenda Brandon had abandoned when she retreated to her hometown of Hopewell to attempt to become just plain Brenda Boynton again.

Charlotte almost regretted that she had accompanied Brenda to Hollywood for a two-week film shoot in a cameo role that Brenda felt her obligation to longstanding movie folk friends would not permit her to turn down. And Charlotte might not have come with Brenda if she had not thought that the companion she had so recently found might be lured back to her Hollywood life if Charlotte weren't there to fight against that. She sensed in Brenda's request that

Charlotte come along that the former movie star too was afraid that might happen. So Charlotte felt only a twinge of guilt that her presence was entirely selfish.

The two women walked into the restaurant of the Hotel Bel-Air in Hollywood. Brenda, the startling beautiful and shapely blonde who was maturing divinely, stood at the entrance into the dining room perhaps a heartbeat too long and then she was being swamped with acquaintances and admirers who all were telling her of their pleasure that she had come back to town. Then she was explaining that it was only temporary, that she wasn't moving back and was just here for a cameo role in a movie she couldn't resist that was being directed by an old friend of hers. Meanwhile, Charlotte, a bit more than a statuesque brunette, with streaks of gray, who was older and more awkward in her carriage and who couldn't say, really, that she was doing more than just aging followed the scraping and bowing maître d' on to the table he had selected for them in the center of the restaurant. Brenda was obviously the biggest celebrity they'd had show for lunch so far that day.

Charlotte didn't begrudge Brenda her celebrity and all of the attention she was getting. She watched everyone tugging at Brenda's sleeve to stop her en route to their table to mutter "look everyone, I know Brenda Brandon" words of welcome. Following this, they looked, curiously, with just a touch of pity and amusement, at Charlotte. At this, the former FBI investigator kept telling herself she was glad she'd come on this trip—it was Brenda who was real and who mattered, not these people. Brenda would turn her brilliant smile and watery blue eyes on each supplicant, giving them a few instances of her undivided attention, and they would melt in the presence of her majesty.

Charlotte was less concerned now that Brenda would be drawn back into the fake swirl that is Hollywood. Brenda was a more genuine person than anyone else Charlotte had encountered here. And knowing Brenda as well as she did,

8

Charlotte could see the mild irritation and impatience churning under Brenda's surface—the impatience to step back out of the limelight and to get back to Hopewell—to return home—and to get back to Sam and Rocket, the dogs the two had acquired in recent mysterious times on the misleadingly calm and sleepy banks of the Choptank.

Finally, Brenda was seated, Charlotte having been able to proceed to their table well before her companion because no one was tugging at her sleeve for attention. The quizzical expressions on the faces around them didn't cease, and Charlotte thought once again that they all no doubt were wondering who this dumpy old broad was that Brenda was sitting with.

"Bear up, Charlotte," Brenda said in the rich, melodious voice of hers that made theatergoers worldwide sigh with pleasure. "It will only be two weeks. I promise. And I'll spend as little time at the studio filming as I can manage."

"I feel like I'm in a filming of the *Fawn and the Cow*," Charlotte answered in a voice she was trying to keep from trembling.

Brenda reached over and placed a hand affectionately on Charlotte's arm and said, "Nothing of the sort." She exchanged a smile with Charlotte that reassured Charlotte that Brenda saw her in an entirely different light and wouldn't trade any of the overdressed, body-sculpted, and plasticized people in the room for a retired FBI investigator.

In looking around—and her well-trained investigator's instincts were still sharp—Charlotte noticed that there was one couple at a table not far from them who, although they too had their attention focused on Brenda, were not in keeping with the furtive, worshipful glances the others in the restaurant were casting Brenda's way. The young woman was looking daggers at Brenda, and the young man with her had a restraining hand on the woman's arm and was whispering to her intensely.

Brenda didn't notice them, however. With shock, she'd picked out an entirely different couple who were the last ones on earth she expected to see—either here or together—or alive, for that matter. Both had been principals in an international scandal mystery Charlotte had been investigating in Hopewell just before the two had come to Hollywood. Brenda hadn't realized the full ramifications of that case, but Charlotte had. Charlotte's skills had enabled her to see the couple as soon as she entered the restaurant. Any shock she might have felt over seeing a man who many thought was dead with a woman that few knew he had any connection to was erased by the speculation Charlotte had already entertained as she had been solving that case. Seeing the couple here gave her the satisfaction of having so many of the loose ends of what she knew as the "Retired with Prejudice" case resolve themselves as soon as she saw the couple.

"Charlotte, you don't seem a bit surprised," Brenda said in sotto voce, herself clearly surprised.

"I'm surprised at the coincidence of seeing them here, yes. But I knew she had come out to California. So, I surmised he was here as well. Don't worry. I'm quite sure the government knows all about it."

Brenda and Charlotte spoke quietly and intently over this "find" for a few minutes—so intently that they didn't notice the flustered young woman approach their table until she was right there, at Brenda's elbow.

"I can't believe you had the nerve to come back here," the woman hissed at Brenda, the belligerence in her voice matching the ugly expression on her face. The young man who had been sitting with her was hovering just behind her and plucking ineffectually at her arms. "But I'm glad you did. They'll get you this time. I'll see that they do."

"Please, Gretchen, not here. Not now. People are watching." The voice was Brenda's. She was not looking at the young woman but, rather, was turning her crystal water glass this way and that, picking up a rainbow of colors from the chandeliers overhead, and using a calm soothing voice.

"Yes, Brenda, people are watching. Just what I want them to do," The young woman hissed, although she said it over her shoulder, because the young man now had her wrapped in his arms and was pulling her away from Brenda and Charlotte's table and toward the restaurant's exit. "And we'll be giving them plenty to watch, you and I," the woman growled as, with the help of the restaurant staff, she was bundled out of the restaurant.

Indeed, all action in the restaurant had stopped during this brief interlude, and all were looking at Brenda and Charlotte's table, their eyes big and luminous, their jaws on their chests and working back and forth, at the ready for their faces to lean into those of their companions and to start assessing what they'd seen in low, excited voices. Charlotte was quick to note that the older couple they had been discussing had disappeared from the room.

"Quite an entrance back into Hollywood, wouldn't you say?" Brenda said, her voice still calm, her body still under complete control. "Ruby Robey will have a field day with this tomorrow."

For anyone who didn't know Brenda as well as Charlotte did, it no doubt looked like Brenda wasn't fazed at all by that little scene. But Charlotte could tell that her companion, under that superb job of acting, had been knocked off her pins and was both embarrassed and concerned. Her cheeks were burning and her eyes were flashing.

"I take it not one of your admirers," Charlotte murmured. She was speaking from behind her menu, like Brenda, trying her best to play like nothing had just happened. "But Ruby Robey? Who's she?"

"Ah, I keep forgetting that you are a Hollywood neophyte. Ruby is the movie colony's very own gossip columnist—not the only one, of course, but the queen bee of the dastardly genre. I knew she'd have quite a good time with my return, but this is a gold mine for her pick and shovel. And me just a small-town girl from Maryland. She'd have a field day with my rural upbringing if she knew about that."

"Hardly a small-town girl, Brenda," Charlotte said, with a laugh. "Your family was probably the most prominent one on the eastern bank of the Chesapeake." But then she stopped talking, remembering that Brenda had once said she was sent away from Hopewell by her father after her mother had been murdered and suspicion had been cast on Brenda.

The women were both silent for a moment, as they pretended to study their menus.

"I should have introduced you to the young woman," Brenda said to end the period of silence. "But she didn't really give me a chance. I have no idea who the nice-looking young man was—and I feel sorry for him being dragged into the middle of this. The young woman was Gretchen Lund. I'll no doubt run across her at the studio again. She's one of the studio's premier makeup artists and a favorite of my film's producer, so it's quite likely she'll be assigned to my movie. But I'm sure they will be sensitive enough not to assign her to do my makeup."

"Is that all?"

"No, obviously not. She's also the daughter of the woman I was living with in Beverly Hills before I left Hollywood, Helga Lund. I have told you about her. The award-winning costume designer."

"And this young woman disapproved of her mother's living arrangements."

"I'm afraid it goes a bit beyond that. Gretchen believes—truly believes, it seems obvious—that I murdered her mother."

Then, as Charlotte looked up from her menu and gave Brenda a sharp look, Brenda continued in a controlled contralto voice, "But enough of that. I see our waiter heading in our direction and I haven't had time to narrow my choice down yet. What do you think? The Cobb salad or bread and water?"

Charlotte knew that there was such a case that had driven Brenda east, of course, but she hadn't remembered the name of the other woman.

"I'd go with the Cobb salad," Charlotte said dryly. "I was thinking of a steak with French fries myself, but perhaps I'd better stick with the shrimp salad."

* * * *

"It was here, in the entrance foyer. I found her swinging from that light fixture. It looks so delicate, doesn't it? She was a small woman. But, still, that was my first thought when I saw her dangling there—that I didn't know why it didn't fall from her weight."

"Brenda, you don't have to do this. We don't have to be here."

"But I think we do, Charlotte. I don't want to hold anything back from you. I told you that Helga and I were living together—that we were lovers. But I didn't tell you everything about how she died—or that I found her. They've officially ruled it suicide, of course, but I have a feeling they still have the books open on it at the Los Angeles Police Department. And I've heard rumors that John Lu is writing a screenplay, which would be strange, as the scenario itself seemed to come from one of his screenplays." Brenda laughed, a hollow laugh that Charlotte didn't like the sound of.

They were standing in the foyer of a small gem of a mansion in the Beverly Hills section above Hollywood. A perfectly proportioned stuccoed house with a mansard roof straight out of a Tuscany vineyard. The entrance foyer was two stories and there was a large window over the front door. When the chandelier was on at night, it would be seen from down on Sunset Boulevard. Charlotte ghoulishly wondered if

13

it had been lit the night Brenda found the body of her companion—whether Hilda Lund had been swinging from that chandelier for hours, in full view of the nightclub district below, but with no one looking up to the house on the hill. Not expecting to find a body swinging on a light fixture if they did look there.

"Brenda—"

"It was a movie that has helped cast suspicion on me," Brenda continued.

She was walking in circles in the hall, looking up at the chandelier. The house was largely unfurnished, and Charlotte found herself placing the furniture that Brenda had brought back to her family Federal-style manse on Hopewell's main street. Everything looked spotless, in white, except for the modern paintings on the wall in a lounge that Charlotte could see to the right and a full, formal dining room to the left off the foyer. The paintings were rendered in large swaths of vibrant color—reminiscent to Charlotte of obscene slashes of lipstick across otherwise pristine white walls. This wasn't Brenda's style, Charlotte didn't think. Other than the Chippendale and Sheraton family heirlooms Brenda had brought to Hollywood, Charlotte thought that it must have been Helga who had done the designing of these interiors. Charlotte was quickly developing the image of a woman who was overdramatic—which also didn't seem to be Brenda's style.

"A movie?" Charlotte couldn't help herself. She was the perpetual sleuth. It had been hypocritical of her to try to get Brenda to not relive this—not to bring Charlotte to the scene of the crime. Of course Charlotte was curious about it all.

"Yes, the movie *Woman Scorned*. Surely you saw it. This . . ." and here Brenda gave a sweeping gesture that took in the chandelier and the surrounding white walls of the foyer ". . . helped that movie set box office records."

"No, I didn't see it," Charlotte answered. "Until I retired, I'm afraid I didn't have much time for the movies."

"Ah, honest Charlotte to the end," Brenda said. "You could have said, I'm sure, that you've seen me in every movie I've been in—and I wouldn't have questioned you about it. But I prefer you this way. In that movie the character who was my husband—David Runion, as usual—had been unfaithful to me with several women. And while my character showed the face of a faithful and perfect wife to the world, I was going around and murdering the women he was making love to. I dispatched the last one by hanging her from a chandelier. It was a role that was completely contrary to anything I'd done before. I think the shock of that alone was what got me nominated for an Academy Award for that movie."

Charlotte said nothing.

"This chandelier. Well, not this specific chandelier. They were afraid it wouldn't hold a swinging body, so they installed a sturdier chandelier here. Ironic, isn't it?" Brenda laughed. "Aaron Woolridge, our producer, who is known for being a skinflint, insisted that my house would be the ideal setting for that scene. I know he was just trying to save money. But how deliciously ghoulish can you get? But what's really ghoulish is that this chandelier did manage to support the body of a woman in real life."

"I see," Charlotte now said. And that's all she said, but her mind was racing. She already was beginning to form a theory on the death of Helga Lund, and she was determined now, more than ever, to stay as close as she could to Brenda's side throughout these two weeks of filming.

"It was all the more titillating because Helga and I hadn't been getting along and we'd had what you could term as a cat fight on the set two days before she died. Helga was interesting that way—quite the drama queen."

"So I've gathered," Charlotte murmured.

Brenda gave her a sharp look but continued. "At first, the gossips were saying that Helga killed herself and then, when the police questioned me and I couldn't give an alibi, the tumblers started to fall into place—at least that's how it seemed to me in the sudden interest the police took."

"Couldn't provide an alibi—or wouldn't?" Charlotte asked. As soon as she'd asked it, she regretted doing so. She hadn't been able to help herself. She had fallen right into her old interrogation habits.

"Let's not go there," Brenda said.

And then Brenda was saved by the bell—or, rather, her cell phone. She withdrew to the arch going into the living room, but no farther. It was as if she didn't want to be impolite in answering the phone while Charlotte was standing there but also didn't want Charlotte to think there was anything in her life closed to the other woman.

When she hung up, she was looking a little quizzical. "That was our lawyer—Helga's and mine; we shared him. For a good many years there we shared nearly everything. He says if I hadn't returned to California, he'd have had to summon me back. He's finally probated Helga's will, he says, and I need to be there for the reading."

"Yes. Why the questioning look, though? That all sounds natural."

"I never thought of Helga as owning anything. And whatever she had I assumed would go to Gretchen, her daughter."

"When's the reading?"

"He says he can do it tomorrow afternoon. But that was our only afternoon before filming starts that we had to explore together. I hate leaving you in the lurch like that. And I certainly can't ask you to come to the reading of the will."

"No, that would be a little insensitive," Charlotte said. And then she laughed. "It will be fine; I'll find something else to do. If we feel like it at the end of the film shooting, we can stay an extra day or two and explore."

Fortuitously, though, when they returned to the hotel, Charlotte found that she had a luncheon engagement of her own the next day. The chief field agent for the FBI in Los Angeles, Santos Caballero, an old friend of Charlotte, had found she was in town and had called to make a lunch date with her—the sooner the better. And now there was no sooner or better than tomorrow.

Later that evening as the two women sat on the terrace of the hotel, wine glasses in hand and enjoying the sunset over the waters of the Pacific, both were in a pensive mood.

"I've wondered why," Charlotte asked, "during all of those years in Hollywood, when so many stars where waltzing through multiple marriages and playing musical beds, you never married. Have you always known you preferred women? Were you with Helga for a long time?"

"No, Helga was fairly recent, and I wasn't sexually active before that. I guess you could say I was married to my career—and that I was waiting for the man I wanted until it became obvious that was never to be."

"A specific man?"

"Yes, of course. As clichéd as it was, I always wanted the leading man of my movies to be the leading man in my life too. I had a crush on David Runion from the first day I saw him on a movie set. We grew up together in the movies—you could say we grew old there, but David never looked my way—at least not seriously. There was a time he hinted that wanted sex, but that was a time when I was holding out for something more permanent—and he never did more than hint about it. He had marriages during those years, but they always seemed to be marriages of convenience to suit the promotion needs of his talent agent. Each time one of his marriages fell through, I was there to help him pick up the pieces. And yet he never really saw me as a mate—he certainly never directly propositioned me. I'm not sure now what I would have done if he had. Eventually there was

Helga, and I was comfortable with her and we often were roomed together on film locations. I guess you could say we just grew together over time."

"And there were no other men—or women—all that time? You didn't fall for the younger actor in so many of your movies—Tony Trice—for instance? I would have thought—"

Whatever Charlotte would have thought was cut off by the sound of glass shattering on the paving blocks of the patio. Brenda was up in a flash and picking up the shards from her wine glass.

"Sorry," she said, "I guess I was getting too mellow out here. The glass just fell out of my hand."

"Careful there," Charlotte said. "Don't get yourself cut on that. I'll go call out someone from inside. They can attend to that—especially at the prices the studio's paying for our room."

"Ironic, really," Brenda said in a small voice.

"What's ironic?" Charlotte responded.

"Shattered glass. Do you know that that is how my character is to meet her demise in this movie? Cutting herself on poison-treated glass shards." Then Brenda shuddered and pulled her shawl tightly around her body. "It suddenly feels as chilly as death out here. Let's go inside, Char. The sun's down now anyway."

Chapter Two

"There, I told you she'd have it in the morning paper."

Charlotte and Brenda were sitting by the fireplace in their Casa Del Mar penthouse suite, enjoying their breakfast. At least they were enjoying their breakfasts until Brenda opened the morning paper to Ruby Robey's movie world gossip column.

"Listen to this, Char."

> *Like Cher, megastar Brenda Brandon appears to be back for at least another encore on a movie career that has gone on forever. Her old flames, Director Howard Holton and leading man for even longer than Brenda's been around, David Runion, have ganged up to bring her back for yet one more death scene. (Oh, my, did I really refer to Brenda and a death scene? Sorry, Brenda. I make no accusations.) But her first appearance in Hollywood upon her return was more like* Family Feud *than* Oedipus Rex. *Despite the hefty female bodyguard she was seen with at the Hotel Bel-Air yesterday, the daughter of Brenda's lost Helga gave her an explosive welcome back in Tinsel Town. If those two knew Helga like I knew Helga . . .*

Brenda stopped reading. She had halted and been reading through clinched teeth for the last two sentences.

"Is that all?" Charlotte asked. "Or would you rather not read more? That would be perfectly fine with me. She does sound like a malicious harpy."

"That's Hollywood for you," Brenda responded in a small voice. "No, I read to the end. Ruby often does that. Just cuts it short and leaves you hanging—makes it sound like she knows so much more dirt than she's telling."

"I don't get the references to *Family Feud* and *Oedipus Rex*, though."

"I guess it's a lame comparison of ensemble movie casts to dysfunctional families," Brenda said in almost a whisper.

Charlotte looked at Brenda and was surprised to see that she was white as a sheet. Charlotte hadn't seen anything affect Brenda like this.

"Still, she's reigned with this sort of crap far too long," Brenda continued. "I could wring her neck."

"Not before tomorrow afternoon, please," Charlotte said sweetly, trying to switch gears on the conversation. "You promised to give me a studio tour before they rev up for your movie, and if you off this gossip columnist we'll have to be making a trip to the police department instead. And I *would* like to see the set. I know they won't let me on the set while you're filming—unless, of course, you can take the hint from this Robey woman and try to pass me off as your bodyguard."

Brenda didn't laugh.

This bothered Charlotte as she rode in a hotel taxi to the Palm restaurant in downtown Los Angeles to meet Santos Caballero for lunch. This wasn't like Brenda. Something in that newspaper column had really put her off her stride. Charlotte was conflicted. She wanted to stay out of Brenda's private business, but she couldn't help but feel that something was very wrong here and that Brenda needed her help.

"Hello, Charlotte. Retirement seems to be very good for you. You look more relaxed and happier than you ever did during those mandatory all-chiefs meeting in Washington."

"Good afternoon, Santos," Charlotte said with a laugh. Caballero had been waiting for her at the hostess' desk. Charlotte had to admit that he looked as stressed as he always had. "I thought it was against the law not to be relaxed in California."

"I wish."

"Business as bad as usual?"

"You could say that. We already have a table. Come this way. There's someone I want you to meet."

Charlotte followed along behind the chief of the L.A. FBI office. He was a good foot taller than she was, and she wasn't a short woman. But she could see that he had put on weight—and there was a limp now. Then she remembered the incident of the terrorists at the airport the year before and how they hadn't gotten to all of the bombs in time and he'd gotten shrapnel in his leg. These were certainly challenging days for the FBI, she thought. And for the umpteenth time in recent months, she was glad that she had retired when she did. Still, she would have missed the investigative work if she hadn't had occasion to continue doing some of that.

She spied the other man as they were coming closer to the table. He obviously was law enforcement but was even more bedraggled and blood-shot-eyed than Caballero was. Local police, Charlotte deduced. But why on earth, she thought, would someone from the LAPD be doing lunching with the FBI? And why did Santos say the man was someone he wanted her to meet?

"Charlotte Diamond, I'd like you to meet Detective Luis Sanchez of the LAPD Homicide Division," Caballeros said. The man stood up in respect and smiled wanly at Charlotte as they were introduced.

"I'm honored, Ms. Diamond," he said "Santos has told me something of your legend in the department on the East Coast, and I stand somewhat in awe of your record."

"Nothing to compare with what you folks have to face on the West Coast, I'm sure," Charlotte said politely as she sat and motioned the men to sit as well. Both of the men were of Hispanic origin, which Charlotte understood was an advantage for them in Los Angeles. But, whereas Caballero could be likened to a mastiff, Sanchez was more a terrier. High strung, always in motion, rather short and slim. He was nearly bald, which Charlotte got the impression was caused by ulcers and a frenetic, worrying nature. But he also gave the impression that he always tenaciously ran his quarry to ground. She didn't think he would be someone she'd want to face as an opponent.

"It's nice meeting you. Santos said just now that we should meet. But I'm afraid I don't—"

"We don't want to beat around the bush, Charlotte," Caballero said. "You came to California with Brenda Brandon, didn't you?"

"Yes we live in the same town as each other in Maryland now. And have become good friends. But I don't know what interest that would be at the LAPD Homicide Division." She was just buying time here to compose herself. She was quite sure she did know what this was about.

"I think there are some things you need to know. Let's order first," Caballero said. "This may take some time. And Luis and I do need to eat lunch. We've both had long days behind us, and I suspect Luis has got as full a day still facing him as I do."

Charlotte welcomed the break. She could not have told anyone what she had either ordered or eaten that day she was so focused on what these men had to say.

Over coffee Caballero nodded to Sanchez and he turned to Charlotte. "You may not know it, but Brenda

Brandon was involved in a murder investigation before she left Hollywood."

"Yes, she did tell me about that. Helga Lund, a woman she worked with and lived with. In fact, yesterday she took me to the house where it happened. Brenda's kept the house, but we're staying at a hotel. She was quite open with me about it."

"Oh? Did she give you an alibi for the time of the . . . death? Because she certainly never has given us one."

Charlotte blanched. They really were getting right down to it. And no, she'd tough it out, but Brenda most definitely had not told her what her alibi was for that time of Helga Lund's death nor why she wouldn't give one to the police.

"Brenda told me that Lund's death was ruled a suicide. Is this not true?"

"Yes, it's true," Sanchez said with a heavy sigh. "This is Hollywood. A star of Brenda Brandon's stature could run amok down Rodeo Drive dispatching tourists left and right with a broadsword and this town would paper it over as mass suicide. No, cases like this never close in Los Angeles. This is the town of make believe. We actually have a law here that allows us to say cases are closed but we keep them in a pending file and can reopen them with just a scrap of new information."

"That must be convenient for you," Charlotte said. "But I know Brenda quite well, and all of my instincts as an investigator tell me she wouldn't do something like this."

"I set this meeting up, Charlotte," Caballero broke in, "because I have a great deal of respect for you. I want to be sure that you understand what the situation is here and are given every opportunity to protect yourself. I know Luis well, too, and I trust his instincts implicitly. He's been on this case since Lund's death, and he tells me he is quite sure that Brenda Brandon is his perpetrator. We're going well out on the limb here in discussing this with you—as I'm sure you are well aware. But we'd really like to have you inside the tent on this rather than outside and conducting your own investigations. So, as irregular as it is, we want to lay our cards on the table about Brenda Brandon."

"How strong of a case do you have?" Charlotte turned to Sanchez and asked. She kept her trembling hands in her lap and tried to put on a neutral face. She was seething with both anger and concern, but she wanted to know all that they suspected, so she wanted to put on as reasonable a front as possible.

"If we could just discern a firm motive, I think we'd be home free. Two women bitching at each other isn't enough for me. I'm sure there's something else there."

I certainly hope not, Charlotte thought. She didn't say it. She knew she should be grateful to these men for giving her this warning. They seemed sure of themselves. They didn't know Brenda like she had come to, but she could see now that she needed to try to step back and look at all of this objectively—not because she now believed Brenda was involved in Lund's death, but because now was the time to get to the truth of the matter, a truth that every instinct told her would exonerate the woman she loved.

Later that afternoon, Charlotte was still sitting in front of the fireplace in their suite trying to think through the issue and to form the questions she needed to find answers for when Brenda returned from the reading of the will.

Charlotte could tell there was something amiss as soon as Brenda entered the suite. The movie actress walked across the floor and nearly fell into the chair by the fireplace across from where Charlotte was sitting. Charlotte had the presence of mind to note that even in such an entrance as this, Brenda Brandon, the actress, was a figure that commanded the complete attention of an audience.

"Well . . . that was . . . strange," Brenda said after she had fought to control her breathing.

"What was strange?" Charlotte asked, almost afraid to hear the answer. "Did it turn out that Helga Lund had something to bequeath after all?"

"Yes. That's what's strange. I have no idea where she got it. There certainly was no evidence of it when she was living with me. Helga was extravagant and she didn't make as much as one might suppose from her costume designing. She was such a perfectionist that I'll bet there was more of her own earnings than studio money in the costumes she conjured up."

"Are you telling me that she left you some money?"

"Over $800,000, yes. Again, I have no idea where Helga got that much money."

"She left it to you and not her daughter? That must have caused an unpleasant scene at the reading of the will."

"Yes, there was a scene. And Gretchen Lund said ugly things about my relationship with Helga that I'll no doubt read in Ruby Robey's column tomorrow. And she's going to challenge the will and sue me, she says, and she wasn't placated when I told her she could have it all if she wanted it. But, no, Helga didn't leave it all to me. She left even more to Gretchen than to me. The woman had accumulated over two million dollars somehow."

Charlotte sat there, speechless. Brenda was seeing this as just something strange and an extension of unpleasantness with Lund's daughter. But Charlotte knew this was so much more. Eight hundred thousand dollars was one hell of a good motive for murder. At least the LAPD would have no trouble seeing it that way.

Chapter Three

Charlotte said nothing else that evening about the issue and the danger she could see Brenda was in. There wasn't much time for such a conversation, anyway, as Brenda had been invited to attend the premier of a Howard Holton film at Grauman's Chinese Theater as his guest, and he had graciously said she could bring Charlotte as well.

Brenda was, of course, radiant throughout the evening, and Charlotte did what she could to withdraw to the shadows—except that Brenda kept taking her by the arm and pulling her back in. Charlotte could see that many a questioning eye was cast on her.

"Please let me stand away from you, Brenda, at least until we get to our seats. Everyone is giving me the evil eye."

"Do you mind terribly, Char?" Brenda asked. "Because, if so, we can go home. But I can tell you that the tongues will be wagging even faster if I show any need to hide you. Would you like to leave? We can go. I'm sure Howard would understand."

"No, of course not. That would be an insult to your host—and you'll be starting to film under his direction the day after tomorrow. I'll manage. I'll try to look as calm and collected as you look, and as if I'm having fun."

"Oh, do you think I'm having fun? I guess I really can act," Brenda said, and she turned to Charlotte and gave her a wondrous smile, and to the flashing of camera lights, she gave

Charlotte an affectionate hug. "I don't want to snub Howard either, and I want you to see the inside of Grauman's. The 'fun' part is all acting, I assure you."

Brenda tightened her hold on Charlotte's arm but didn't break her smile when a voice was heard from the crowd bordering the red carpet leading into the theater, "Come back to face the music on Helga Lund, Brenda?"

The crowd jabbered and hissed, and a second voice cried out, "We love you, Brenda," but the moment was over quickly and the women continued their stroll through the throngs and into the theater—if at a bit faster pace than right after they'd descended from the studio limousine.

The evening went up hill from there. Charlotte found the interior of the theater to be gorgeous and everyone to be polite to her because she was in the company of a box office smash actress who had been away for some time. But then when they heard that Charlotte had been a senior FBI investigator, most of them became fascinated and wanted to engage her in conversation. Before the movie even started, the producer Aaron Woolridge—who would also be producing the film Brenda was in—was trying to sign Charlotte up as a movie consultant.

And, of course, when the movie started and afterward while Holton and Wooldridge and the leads in the film were standing on stage and speaking about the film, attention was off Brenda and Charlotte. Now that Brenda was out of the spotlight, no matter how briefly, Charlotte could feel her companion's breathing returning to normal as they sat arm against arm in their theater seats.

En route home in the back of the studio car, Charlotte could feel the tension drain out of her companion and the weariness set in. Brenda leaned her head on Charlotte's shoulder and closed her eyes and Charlotte took Brenda's hand in hers.

"Glad that's over," Brenda muttered, almost making Charlotte start in surprise. She would have guessed that

Brenda had dozed off. "It had to be done, but I'm glad it's over."

"I thought it was a very good movie," Charlotte answered.

"Yes, the movie was fine. I was referring to the first contact with the public since returning to Hollywood. I was dreading that."

"One wouldn't have known that by the way you were carrying yourself."

"Thanks. I don't think I could have done it without you by my side. I know this trip West is trying for you, but having you here is a great help to me."

"I'm glad you see it that way." Charlotte almost went on to say something else, but now it seemed that Brenda really had nodded off, and Charlotte didn't disturb her, knowing that Brenda had not slept well the previous night and not wanting to rob her of any sleep she could get. Charlotte contemplated, in horror, what would be happening to Brenda—what the LAPD homicide detective would be putting her through and she would have had to face alone—if Charlotte hadn't come. Charlotte couldn't stop the investigation, but her mere presence made the investigators tread carefully.

In the car on the way to the studio the next day, though, Charlotte decided she needed to say something. She didn't want Brenda to learn from anyone else that she had met with the detective on Helga's death investigation.

"My lunch with my FBI colleague yesterday had a surprising twist to it, Brenda."

"Oh?"

"Yes, an LAPD homicide detective, Luis Sanchez, was there."

"Ah, yes. I should have guessed that Mr. Sanchez would pull you aside. Told you not to turn your back on me, did he?"

"Something like that, yes. Did you know that the investigation was being held open?"

"Yes, I would have guessed that it had. It was the downside to coming back here. As long as I was on the other coast I could fantasize that none of this existed."

"The sticking point seems to be your alibi and your unwillingness to provide one. But I suppose you know that."

"Yes," Brenda answered with a heavy sigh.

"And you have good reason for not providing one?"

"I think so, yes."

"Good enough to be willing to remain under a cloud?"

Brenda didn't answer. Charlotte didn't really need for her to. Brenda was an intelligent woman. She knew what she was sacrificing by not answering. So, Charlotte assumed that her reason overshadowed the risk of not telling. Charlotte changed gears. If she was going to believe in Brenda, she was going to have to pursue other avenues.

"You were surprised at the size of Helga's estate. Were her daughter and she close?"

"No, they were estranged. Gretchen was always the angry woman—well, you saw her at the restaurant. There was no husband in the picture, and Helga refused to tell Gretchen who her father was. That produced a great tension between the two. Anger was normal for Gretchen. Every time she and her mother came in contact—which was unavoidable as they worked for the same studio—there would be explosions. And they were always caused by Gretchen. I'm not surprised that Helga left her all that money, though. The separation wasn't really forced or fomented from Helga's side. Her position was that Gretchen would be diminished rather than satisfied by knowing who her father was. Helga thought she was protecting Gretchen. She always spoke with pride about her daughter when she mentioned Gretchen to me—and she didn't avoid talking about Gretchen."

"It's the surprise that interests me. Did Gretchen seem surprised that there was so much money at stake? I got the impression when you were telling me about what happened in the lawyer's office that she wasn't."

"No, she didn't seem surprised at the amount at all—just that I was being bequeathed nearly half of it."

"And yet you, who were living with Helga, didn't know she had that much money when her estranged daughter seemed to know it. That's what I find a little surprising."

"Oh, I see what you mean," Brenda answered.

"Perhaps I'll have an opportunity to talk to Gretchen about that."

"Perhaps so, if she's working today. And here we are at the gates to the inner sanctum of the studio. Now, please don't shrink away. You've met Howard and Aaron, but I want you to meet the rest. Today's gathering is just a measuring up of each other—and tonight we'll all be meeting at Howard's again to compare how well we can hold our liquor and our tongues."

Charlotte was overwhelmed by the number of people she was introduced to at the studio that afternoon. She'd had no idea that it took so many to put together a production.

Brenda had already told her that this was to be an art film, taking the "bone structure" of the classic Cinderella story, transforming it to the waning days of the Austro-Hungarian empire, and twisting it so the "Cinderella" character was a princess. In this version, it was the princess who fell for a coachman at a ball where she was supposed to be shopping for a husband among the eligible bachelors of the noble families. And a major twist was how her mother tried to help her find her true love and was murdered by a wealthy widowed duchess who was going for a double wedding—her son to the princess and herself to the king. The working title for the film was *The Crystal Ball*, named for the ball held for the princess to select a mate. No one expected the title to hold through the production, though.

The real twist of the movie was in what the director Howard Holton called an inspirational idea to cast Brenda Brandon as the original queen, not revealing in the trailers or publicity that she is murdered early in the film.

This was a familiar ensemble movie in which the theatergoer would expect stereotyped roles. Brenda was frequently matched with David Runion as her leading man, and he would be playing the part of the king in this production. Julie Javetts, who was often the "other woman" in the Brandon and Runion films but who always before lost out to Brenda with the leading man, was playing the duchess. Tony Trice, the perpetual younger, heartthrob actor in the ensemble films, was cast as the sought coachman. DeeDee Yance, known better just as DeeDee, was a teenage singing sensation who was brought in for her first film to play the part of the princess and, more important, to bolster the publicity and box office and help secure financing for the film.

When Charlotte was being reintroduced to Howard Holton and the film's producer, Aaron Woolridge, Holton spoke at great length about how happy and fortunate they all were that he had managed to lure Brenda back for the film.

"In conjunction with DeeDee's appearance, we'll be covering three decades of fan interest; it will guarantee packed houses," Holton said to Charlotte. "But I am still flabbergasted she came back. She's resisted every other script I've sent her."

"I told him that it was because it was just a cameo appearance even though I get top billing in the publicity," Brenda said with a fabulous smile. "But the truth is that I can't resist the chance to wear the costumes from that era."

"What I haven't told Brenda yet," Woolridge picked up the thread of discussion, "Was that we hadn't cast all the parts before Brenda said yes—all we had was DeeDee, the movie having been selected for her debut. Howard wasn't showing much interest, Tony was on the fence and asking for more money than he finally accepted, and Julie had accepted the original queen's role, but then salivated at the opportunity to play the duchess once Brenda had accepted the queen's role. She said she'd kill to be set off against Brenda in this way. If Brenda hadn't—"

"Excuse me. Ms. Brandon?"

It was a tentative, quiet voice, but it was enough to stop Woolridge in midsentence. The producer turned and looked down his nose at the young man who had interrupted him. Obviously this was something that wasn't often done on the set. Here hierarchy reigned. And someone obviously was not following protocol.

Both Brenda and Charlotte turned to look at the young man who had spoken—and both recognized him immediately as the man who had been with Helga's daughter, Gretchen, in the restaurant where Gretchen had made a scene.

"I'm sorry for interrupting," he stammered, clearly cowed by the look Woolridge was giving him—but he plowed on. "I . . . I want to apologize for the other day, Ms. Brandon. Gretchen isn't really like that. She's not herself. She's just so distressed about what her mother was—"

"Bruce!" The angered yell carried out over the set and everyone turned to see Gretchen Lund standing outside the door to the makeup room.

The young man took on a look of panic and turned and fled in the opposite direction from Gretchen. Giving all a look of challenge and disdain, Gretchen turned and disappeared back beyond the door to her domain.

"Who . . . who was that?" Charlotte asked.

"Gretchen Lund. Makeup," Howard Holton answered in a distracted voice.

"No, I mean the young man," Charlotte said.

"Ah. That was Bruce Frazier, our props man. He's Gretchen's young man. And they usually are a lot less distracting than this. But, come, it's time for you to meet the rest of our jolly little crew."

David Runion was gentlemanly and a bit histrionic and over-the-top in his sweeping bow and kissing of Charlotte's hand, and Julie Javetts was somewhat the opposite, giving Charlotte a weak-handed shake and backing away from her and looking at her speculatively, as Charlotte surmised she did for any woman in any room she entered. The woman reeked of stale cigarette smoke, and Charlotte was delighted when she backed away. Charlotte imagined that Brenda had found her an irritant and handful in earlier films, but Brenda was being gracious and friendly to her now—no doubt driving the other woman to distraction. This, of course, would be Brenda's reward for having to put up with the icy enmity.

DeeDee Yance wasn't on the set. She was being represented right up to filming by her mother, Helen, a typical stage mother, who both the director and producer were avoiding as much as possible and who they didn't bother to introduce either Charlotte or Brenda to.

"And this is our beautiful young man actor, Tony Trice," Holton said, pulling a handsome blond man into the circle. Charlotte turned, holding out her hand, and almost melted as she looked into his pale blue eyes and took in the smile he gave her. She almost blurted out her surprise but was caught short—to her great relief later—when Holton caught her attention to introduce her to another man.

"And this is our scriptwriter, John Lu. He's been with Aaron and me through many a motion picture—and Brenda and David as well."

Charlotte almost completely forgot Tony Trice when she turned to greet the scriptwriter. Her eyes narrowed and she had to control her response. They talked briefly, but Charlotte later couldn't remember much of what they'd said to each other. Her mind was racing the whole time, needing to leave the set and make some phone calls. And she hoped

33

that Lu hadn't seen anything unusual in how she had reacted to being introduced to him.

Brenda could see that Charlotte was disconcerted and when the others had drifted away from them, she asked her in a low voice, "Have you had enough of this for this afternoon?"

"I'm afraid so. By all means, stay here. I know you have work to do this afternoon. I'll have another chance to talk with your colleagues later, at Mr. Holton's party. I can take a cab back to the hotel."

"Nonsense. The car can take you back and return in plenty of time for me. Why don't you take a nap? You look a little down."

"No, I'm fine," Charlotte answered. "I just have something on my mind that needs to be cleared up. You take care of yourself here, though. Your colleagues seem like a congenial bunch, but I imagine that just below the surface some of them are piranhas."

Brenda laugh. "You certainly are able to assess a situation quickly. That's just one aspect of the fish bowl we all swim in in Hollywood."

Charlotte watched Brenda walk off with David Runion toward two card tables set up in tandem in the center of the set, where the other actors and the director and scriptwriter were congregating. Then, not waiting until she got back to the hotel, she stood outside the door to the sound studio and used her cell phone to call Santos Caballero, at his L.A. FBI office.

"Santos. It's Charlotte. There's something I need for you to do for me. I need to have someone checked out . . . yes, it might relate to the Lund case. But, if I'm right, it relates to something a whole lot bigger than that."

* * * *

Howard Holton's party that night was a much more inclusive one than Brenda had thought it would be. In the crush of the crowd not long after they'd gotten there, she whispered to Charlotte that if she'd known that the guest list would include media columnists and photographers with their flashing bulbs and a bevy of sweaty-handed financial backers for the films, some of whom could be cast in a New Jersey Mafia movie themselves, she would have declined the offer. They were working their way toward the exit when, as happens sometimes at these massive gatherings, for some reason everyone stopped talking at the same time—except for one person.

That one person, the gossip columnist Ruby Robey, who was quite drunk and was slurring her words, had chosen that moment to tug on Brenda's arm and declare in a loud voice, "You think you knew Helga. But you didn't know Helga as well as I did. If you only knew what Helga and I could . . ."

There undoubtedly was more to that sentence, and Charlotte actually regretted she didn't hear the rest, all of her instincts as an investigator having screamed to her that the columnist had some very telling information to convey. But Brenda had kept on moving, and at that moment the noise of the crowd filtered back in and Ruby Robey's speech was drowned out.

This was the only moment that Charlotte actually remembered from the short time they spent at Howard Holton's party, because five hours later Ruby Robey was dead.

When they returned to the hotel, Brenda had declared that she was keyed up and had been overwhelmed with the presence of people that day and that, if Charlotte didn't mind, Brenda would take a walk on the beach to gather her thoughts.

Charlotte would have liked to walk with Brenda. Here she was on the West Coast, facing a beach, and she hadn't been on the beach yet. But she knew that Brenda was politely trying to convey that she needed some time entirely to herself. So, Charlotte said, "Yes, you go ahead and take your walk. I'm much too tired to go out again. All I want to do is to get out of these clothes and this tight girdle and drop on the bed."

She didn't immediately do that, though. She took a long steamy bath and then laid in bed in the light of the lamp on the bedside table and read a mystery novel and periodically looked at the telephone beside her, willing it to ring—which it didn't do. Eventually, she became too drowsy to read the print in the book, and she turned off the light and drifted off to sleep.

It had been much more than an hour and Brenda hadn't returned to the room before Charlotte went to sleep.

Sometime later, she was awakened by the sound of the telephone ringing. She turned first to see that Brenda was in the bed beside her before she looked at her clock and saw that it was four in the morning. Then she answered the telephone, figuring that a call at this time meant her hunch had been correct.

But the call wasn't the one Charlotte had been expecting.

"Hello. Ms. Diamond?"

"Yes," Charlotte answered, not recognizing the voice—knowing, though, that it wasn't any of the possible voices she had been expecting to hear.

"Sorry to disturb you, but can you tell me where Brenda Brandon is? Oh, sorry, this is Luis Sanchez, LAPD Homicide. We met the other day."

"Yes, I remember. And Brenda's in her bed. Why—?"

"Are you sure? Could you go check to make sure, please."

"Yes, I'm sure," Charlotte said. "She's right here beside me."

"Oh."

Charlotte could tell from his answer that he had had no idea how close the relationship was between her and Brenda. She wanted to laugh. But she suspected that a call from an LAPD Homicide detective at this time of the morning was no laughing matter. And she was right.

"Well, Santos Caballero has suggested that you might come over here—he says he thinks the best way to convince you of what is what is by including you in everything."

"I don't understand. Come over where?"

"Oh, sorry. Come over to Ruby Robey's house—you know, the movie gossip woman. Her house isn't far from your hotel. I can send a man over to get you over here if you like."

"What's the issue, Mr. Sanchez? Let's start over with that. Why do you want me to come over there?"

"She's dead. Ruby Robey got her head bashed in on her front door stoop. Word was from some folks at a party she just left that she and Brenda Brandon had words at the party."

"They most certainly did not," Charlotte said. She was already sitting on the side of the bed and slipping her feet into slippers. "Yes, please send a man over to the hotel. I'll meet him in the lobby. But I can attest that I was right beside Brenda at the party tonight. We didn't stay long. And there was no argument between her and Ruby Robey."

When she'd hung up the phone and started to dress, Brenda apparently being dead to the world on her side of the bed, Charlotte hoped she had given that answer to Sanchez convincingly. There hadn't been an altercation, but Ruby Robey had said something to Brenda, and Charlotte had seen that it was something Brenda didn't like hearing. All she could think of, though, was that he said that Ruby Robey lived near the hotel—and that Brenda had been gone unexpectedly long on her beach walk.

Charlotte felt guilty, but the investigator in her sent her looking in the closet for the clothes and shoes Brenda had been wearing when she left for her walk. Charlotte breathed at least a partial sigh of relief when she saw that there was sand in the soles of the shoes Brenda had worn and that the blouse and slacks Brenda had put on to take her walk were a bit damp and smelled of the salty sea. At least that much was true. She'd have to be honest with herself, though. She needed to see where Ruby Robey's house was in relationship to the sea and the hotel.

Chapter Four

"What have you found there, Ms. Diamond?"

"A ledger and a bankbook."

"Anything interesting in them?" the detective asked.

Charlotte was at the crime scene—Ruby Robey's house—which thankfully wasn't on the beach, but not so thankfully was within a twenty-minute walk of the hotel. Charlotte knew for a fact that Brenda had been gone from the hotel for well over the forty minutes it would take her to walk to the house and return.

"I'd say yes. I and others will need to give them a better look, but I've seen this before—not as tidily kept together, though. Ruby Robey obviously didn't expect anyone to be going through her desk. When I put them together, the ledger looks like it's reporting income from various sources, represented by initials, and the bank book looks like bank deposits of these funds and then a division of the money— just to one other person."

"Anyone we know?"

"I don't know. But there are only two bank accounts receiving money. I trust one of them is Ruby's account and the other one is for someone else. Here, you can obtain the account holders' names, I'm sure. Significant amounts too. They go up into the millions each, even divided."

Charlotte sat down at the desk and started reading the double initials entered there: HK, BX, II, KK, UU, ES, among others. She wondered what they stood for. They were strange initials to be representing names. But maybe there was some sort of code in play.

"Detective," she said, looking up at the man, who, wearing rubber gloves, was still, along with a couple of police officers, examining everything in the room closely. "Could you call Detective Sanchez into the room? I think he'll want to see this."

The detective looked a little embarrassed. "Detective Sanchez isn't here, ma'am. He, uh . . . got another call nearly a half hour ago and went off on that."

"Another call? He's working another case as well?"

"Uh, no. Same case. Over at the movie set—the new Brenda Brandon movie."

"Why has he gone there?"

"There's been another murder there this morning. We think it may be related to—"

Charlotte didn't listen for the end of the sentence. She was up out of the chair at the desk and headed for the door. If none of the policemen here would drive her over to the studio, she'd call a cab—but pity any of the policemen here who stood in her way in getting to the studio immediately.

* * * *

"Are you OK?"

"Yes, yes, I'm fine. It was just such a shock. I found him, you know."

"What happened? How did he die? Do you know?" Charlotte asked. She was in Brenda's dressing room, crouched over her companion, who was sitting at her dressing table, yards and yards of material from her satin period costume fanning out around her. There was a golden crown encrusted with glass stones sitting lopsidedly on her head, and Charlotte gently released the pins holding it there and took it off Brenda's head and laid it the dressing table.

She smoothed Brenda's hair back in place before she let Brenda continue.

They had started the movie filming with her scenes, Brenda then said. She had told Holton and Woolridge that she was finding being back in Hollywood was just too stressful for her, and they had promised to film her cameo bits early and, they hoped, to be able to release her before the two weeks they had put her under contract.

"Yes . . . it's so awful. It was how I am supposed to die in the movie. Cut by bits and pieces of a shattered mirror that the duchess character smeared on the cut edges with a poison. There wasn't supposed to be any poison on the prop mirror shards, of course, and the edges weren't really supposed to be sharp enough to cut. Bruce was the props man, so he was in charge of all that. But the police are saying that he died so quickly that there must really have been poison on the edges. They've sent the pieces of glass off to their lab for testing."

Before their conversation went any further, Detective Sanchez was ushered into the dressing room. He gave a look at Charlotte that she recognized as a signal to leave the room, but, although she backed off to the side, she stayed. She didn't like any of this.

"Ms. Brandon, I'm Detective Sanchez. I believe you were the last one to see the victim alive. Could you tell me exactly what you saw and when?"

"Ah, I can, yes. But I've already given a statement a couple of—"

"Yes, but I will have a couple of related follow-on comments too. For instance, is it not true that you also had an altercation with the gossip columnist Ruby Robey at a party last evening, and was there any time in the night when—?"

Brenda looked like a deer in the headlights and Charlotte stepped forward and said, somewhat exasperated, "Detective Sanchez, I have already told you that I was with

41

Brenda the whole time at the party last evening and that there was no altercation. And has it not occurred to you that if there was poison on those mirror shards Bruce Frazier cut himself on, that he quite probably was not the intended victim? It was Brenda who was supposed to handle those shards during the filming."

"Yes, of course, that's a possibility. But—"

"What I think," Charlotte overrode him, "Is that Brenda really should have her counsel here before she goes any further with this interview."

Sanchez shot Charlotte a look of contemplation and assessment rather than anger—which concerned Charlotte more than if he had shown pique at her intervention.

"Very well, Ms. Diamond," he said. "But perhaps you might obtain counsel too. I have a few more questions for you about your activities last night as well."

"Fine, Detective," Charlotte answered. "I'm sure the studio can recommend one for me. But while we're waiting for them to arrive, perhaps you and I should have a little chat about what I found at Ruby Robey's house and how that might fit into the investigation here."

Sanchez's eyes narrowed.

Good, Charlotte thought. That has put him a bit off his stride.

Ten minutes later, Sanchez and Charlotte were sitting at a card table in the sound studio at the edge of the set, looking coolly at each other and waiting for the items Charlotte specified should be sent over from the Ruby Robey crime scene to arrive, while the bustle of the movie filming tried to regain its momentum around them. Sanchez had already apologized for his loss of control when he suggested that Charlotte obtain a lawyer and had said he knew that she didn't really need one. He didn't say that Brenda didn't need one, though.

While they sat, there was little need to talk, as they had "gone to the movies." Charlotte didn't think she'd ever get over the amount of dramatics that went on outside of the filming on a movie set. If she hadn't come to know Brenda closely, she wouldn't have believed that any of these movie people could retreat from their acting roles.

At first, a bawling Gretchen Lund stormed across the set, headed for Brenda's dressing room door and screaming about Brenda having murdered her Bruce, just like she'd done to her mother. Sanchez already had a couple of policemen posted near Brenda's door, so that storming of the bastion was fairly easily prevented, and the production's doctor had waddled off toward wherever they'd taken Gretchen to give her a sedative. Aaron Woolridge was busy—noisily and imperially so—in trying to drum up makeup artists to take up the slack caused by Gretchen's sudden nonavailability and cracking the whip over Bruce Frazier's assistant props man to make up for Bruce's untimely exit.

The director, Howard Holton, and the two male leads, Tony Trice and David Runion, were on the set going over the scene that Holton was trying to substitute for Brenda's death scene, which most certainly wouldn't now be shot today.

Holton was bellowing in a voice that carried over the general din of the scurrying production crew, "Where's the scriptwriter? Where's John Lu? We need some help here on the lines in this scene." But no one claimed to know where John Lu was. Holton went over to Woolridge and the two had an animated conversation that didn't seem to satisfy either one of them, and then they veered off in different directions again.

Charlotte excused herself at this moment to go to the ladies room, but where she went instead was out into the lane running beside the sound studio, and when she returned she was looking grim but not quite as confused as she had been before.

The real drama came when DeeDee Yance and her mother, Helen, and a bevy of hangers on and studio "suits" arrived a couple of hours after DeeDee's set call and then, having found they had dropped into a real-life death scene, were quickly scuttled away again by Helen to the curses of Howard Holton, who then was rummaging through the script to find some scene that he could do on this day.

Woolridge, feeling the dollars tick away from a production budget that was in full expense mode but without any production, dropped his concern about makeup and props at this point—a wise move, as they now had no idea what scene they were making up for or needing props for—and took up the "Where's John Lu? Where's the scriptwriter?" cry.

Sitting at yet another table, smiling sweetly to herself, and obviously loving every nuance of what was going on, the actress Julie Javetts smoked cigarette after cigarette and preened herself in a nearby full-length mirror.

Sanchez's head seemed to be set on a swivel. He was looking every way at once, with his eyes glittery and his jaw dropped to his chin. Charlotte wished that he was able to see beyond Brenda as the sole suspect in anything, because she was fairly sure he was smart enough otherwise to be gathering some valuable insights into this crowd.

But at last the ledger and bankbook Charlotte had found in Ruby Robey's desk had been delivered and Charlotte and Sanchez were huddled over that and trying to figure out how—and if—it fit into any of these deaths.

So engrossed were they in their speculation—and Charlotte was heartened that Sanchez was being completely open to discussion of possibilities—that neither one of them noticed before he spoke that Tony Trice had broken off from his script meeting and drifted over near them until he almost had his nose in their business.

"Did I hear you say those documents were from Ruby Robey's desk? I think I can tell you what they are."

Both Charlotte and Sanchez looked up in surprise— as surprised that Trice was standing there beside them and

44

listening to them as that he had spoken. So surprised were they that neither spoke before he did so again.

"Those are probably her records of evil," he said. And then he laughed. "She and Helga have been blackmailing half of the people in Hollywood. They've been doing it for years. Undoubtedly they had something on everyone in this film team."

"And you know this because?" Sanchez asked in a low voice, his eyes boring in on Trice's casual smile.

"Why, because they tried to blackmail me too—and succeeded. But just for the one payment. I don't know how Bruce Frazier fits into this, but I'll bet it won't be hard to pick someone—probably a great number of someones—out of that little book there who would be happy to have done either or both of them in."

And now his voice turned hard. "But, if you think you'll find Brenda Brandon's name in there anywhere, I think you're badly mistaken. I wouldn't even try if I were you."

Chapter Five

"You seem to be a little cavalier about this," Detective Sanchez was saying as he, Charlotte, and the young actor, Tony Trice, settled down in the office Aaron Woolridge had had carved out for himself in a corner of the sound studio. Upon Trice's revelation, which had stopped activity on the set and attracted panicked expressions from more than one of the film team working nearby, Sanchez had, wisely, Charlotte thought, asked for a more private place in which to question the young actor. "Could you please tell us what you know of this ledger and how you come to know it?"

"As I said, it doesn't surprise me that Ruby was keeping a ledger. How would you think she'd be able to spill the gossip on the powerful in Hollywood and still keep her position in the hierarchy? It's because she didn't spill the juiciest tidbits of what she knew. She used it to blackmail people. Sometimes she did it for money, sometimes to maintain and enhance her position. Often for the dirt on other people. It was an activity that kept on giving. And she wasn't in it alone. Helga Lund was in it up to her neck as well."

"And, again, you know this how?"

"Because she and Helga tried to blackmail me too—they both contacted me about a secret from my past. I have no real power around here, so they wanted money. And I paid them $10,000. Once. And when they came back for more, I knew they would keep coming back, so I called their bluff and told them to go to hell. They didn't use what they knew, but at that point I didn't care if they did. With what other people are known to be up to here in Tinsel Town, I decided it would only enhance my film image."

"I'm afraid you'll have to tell me what it was they had on you and we'll check your story and start working back from there. We can't rule out that you are covering for something more serious and that you feel so free about it now because you fixed your problem yourself."

"No problem. It may mean I—"

"Stop right there," Charlotte broke in. To this point she'd been sitting off to the side. "I'm surprised Detective Sanchez hasn't mentioned this, but if you are going to be saying anything that will incriminate yourself, you need to consider asking for a lawyer to be present from this point." She turned to Sanchez and gave him a direct stare that made him cringe a bit. What she was hoping, though, was that it would prevent Trice from saying something she feared he'd say that would move Brenda right back into the center of Sanchez's sights.

But then Trice continued as if he hadn't heard her, and what he said came as a great relief to Charlotte. "I had a rough youth. Back in Maryland. I ran with sort of a gang and I was arrested for car theft and jumped bail and came out here. Somehow Ruby and Helga got hold of that information. What they didn't know, though" . . . Trice laughed here . . . "is how we do things in rural Maryland. The books may still be open on that in Annapolis, but I came out here and made good, and I got the word more than a year ago that my family had smoothed everything over. There isn't any paperwork to find anymore on that case even if someone back there wanted to take up the cause. So, for me, having a 'risen from a bad boy past' would now be as useful in publicity as a cover article in *Parade Magazine*."

"You say you made one payment of $10,000 and just that," Charlotte asked. "Do you know about when that was made?"

"Oh sometime in May of last year, I think."

"Let's see," Charlotte said and she took the ledger from Sanchez's hand and started flipping pages. Sanchez leaned in over the book too, knowing what she was looking for. "Aha, right there. It was April, though—$10,000, the initials UU, and," she hesitated as she paged through the rest of the ledger, "I don't see those initials anywhere else."

"Yeah, I guess it was in April. Late April, though. They caught me right after we returned from Africa during filming for my last movie."

"Yes, late April it is. And it looks like he has given us the key to the ledger, Detective Sanchez."

Sanchez looked quizzically at Charlotte—but only for a moment and then he smiled. "The initials. A simple code. They just went up one letter on each initial."

"Yes, it looks that way. And looking through the rest of the pages, we can start picking out other people on the film team who might have been blackmail subjects—and some for much larger sums than Tony paid, and continued to pay too. There, II could be Howard Holton, and KK, Julie Javetts. BX would be Aaron Woolridge; KM, John Lu; and ES, David Runion. It looks like they might have had their claws into nearly the whole film complement. No CG for Bruce Frazier or HK for Gretchen Lund, or," Charlotte said with a bit of triumph in her voice, "CC for Brenda Brandon."

"Interesting, of course, but it might be all a coincidence," Sanchez said. And then he turned to Trice and asked, "You said you knew Brenda Brandon's name wouldn't be in this ledger. How do you—?"

"More than just one coincidence, if so," Charlotte said, overriding Sanchez.

He turned to her now, his eyes narrow, his attention refocused. "What do you mean?"

"I know of another person connected with the film who was a very good candidate for blackmail and whose initials are in this ledger, with his name set against pretty hefty payments."

"Who?"

"Those initials KM. John Lu, the scriptwriter."

"What do you know about that?"

"I recognized him immediately when I saw him on the set the other day—or certainly thought I did. I called the FBI to check him out, and, luckily they did so before he could take off. I panicked there a bit when they were looking for him on the set just a bit ago and he couldn't be found. But when I called Santos Caballero, I alerted him to the possibility Lu was on the wing—and just as we came in here, Caballero called to let me know they'd nabbed him at the airport. He was ticketed for Hong Kong."

"But what—?"

"He's been leading a double life. We knew him on the East Coast as Edward Chang. If Ruby and Helga had their claws in him, they had a real humdinger of a hold. He apparently has been leading a double—or triple—life. Here he's a well-known scriptwriter—well known for his product, not that scriptwriters appear that much in public. But on the East Coast, he was an agent of the Chinese government, targeted against servicemen and employees at the Goddard Space Center, and collecting military and space program secrets from low-level soldiers and technicians. Many of them were of Chinese descent and could be forced to cooperate with Chang—our Lu here—if they still had families in China. Brenda had told me he traveled a lot to the East Coast, but she didn't know that just alerted me further that he was someone who has been on the FBI's watch list for years. He'd just appear and strike and then disappear again before we could touch him."

"OK, so that helps verify what Ruby and Helga were up to and might help explain why they were killed—although just because Brenda's name wasn't in the book doesn't mean she isn't involved. Maybe they just didn't put her name in the book. Or maybe, as close as she was to Helga, she's the surviving member of the blackmail ring and has just cut her partners out of the take."

"Or maybe one of the blackmail victims had enough of being fleeced," Charlotte said impatiently. "The bankbook indicates the take was only split two ways. And Lu has a gigantic motive. Maybe others had motives and opportunity that were just as telling."

"Maybe."

"Maybe we should ask them, then," Charlotte said, jutting her chin out.

"We will. But what would this have to do with Bruce Frazier's death?"

"Oh, I can answer that," Tony Trice said with a dazzling smile.

Both Sanchez and Charlotte turned and looked at him, somewhat surprised to find that he was still in the room as focused as they were on their investigative approach to the issue.

"He almost spilled the beans to you yesterday on the set, Ms. Diamond. He was about to reveal that Helga was a blackmailer—probably Ruby as well. But Gretchen screamed him down."

"And how would he have known that?" Sanchez asked.

"Because he lived with Gretchen and she wears her heart and worries on her sleeve. If she knew about Helga, he would have known too. And if he knew and told you this in the presence of whoever killed Helga and Ruby, he was a prime candidate for murder as well. Knowing about the blackmail scheme would be—and apparently was—what started unraveling all of this."

Both Sanchez and Charlotte looked a bit sheepish. This young man was steps ahead of them. And he just stood there and smiled his beautiful smile and gazed at them with his compelling watery blue eyes.

"Then maybe Brenda wasn't the target of the attack this morning at all," Charlotte said with a sigh of relief.

"Maybe we need to get the Lund girl in here to talk to as well," was what Sanchez said.

"If you want more evidence that there was a blackmail scheme, I think I can tell you what David Runion was being blackmailed for," Trice said, still smiling, like he was enjoying this immensely. And once again, Sanchez and Charlotte swiveled their heads to him in surprise. "You did include his name from the ledger, didn't you?"

"Yes," Charlotte answered, grateful that the query was moving even farther from Brenda.

"He started in the movies in porn—gay male porn. I think his film name was something like Hairy Eight. I doubt that would go over very well with his movie image. He's about at the end of his run anyway; having his early film career involuntary coming out in the open would knock him right out of the movies, I would imagine."

"And how do you know this—that he worked in gay pornographic films?" Sanchez asked in a guarded voice.

"Because he's hit on me from time to time. And he told me about who he was and why he did well in those movies. He bragged about it until I turned him down. And I'll admit I stringed him along on possibilities until my own film career was solidified."

"OK, it's about time to talk to these others," Sanchez said. "Thank you, Mr. Trice. You've been quite helpful. I think you can go home now, if you wish."

"Can I stay around and watch the fireworks, if I wish?" Trice asked. Still those laughing eyes.

"Suit yourself." Sanchez got up and walked to the door. But when he opened it, one of the detectives was there, ready to knock.

"There's a broad downstairs who says she wants to talk to whoever's in charge of this investigation, Luis."

"Is she connected to the film people?"

"I don't think so. She says she's an insurance investigator."

She introduced herself as Rita Sapir, with California Life, when she was ushered in and Tony Trice was being ushered out. She was a fairly good-looking woman, if trying a bit too hard to hang onto her thirties, and Charlotte noticed that she and Tony shared a quick assessment and a smile when she entered the room. She looked all business in a skirt suit and silk blouse, but she also looked like she could let her hair down for clubbing fast enough.

It was her no-nonsense, all-business demeanor, though that impressed, and ultimately slightly distressed, Charlotte.

"What can we do for you, Ms. Sapir?" Sanchez asked when she'd sat down in the chair Trice had just vacated, crossed her trim legs, and smoothed out the skirt of her suit. "I'm afraid we are involved in a murder investigation here, and if your business doesn't connect with that—"

"It very well might be connected," Sapir cut in. "I understand the deceased this morning was a man named Bruce Frazier."

"That's right," Sanchez said, all ears now.

"He isn't what sent me over here today—I was coming anyway, to speak with Ms. Brenda Boynton. But before I left the office, I heard a report on his death on the radio and it rang a bell with me, and I did some checking."

"Brenda Boynton?" Sanchez asked.

"That's Brenda Brandon's real name," Charlotte offered in a small voice. It pained her to provide that information, but she was sure that would be revealed by Rita Sapir within moments anyway.

"Yes, the same," Sapir said. "I was coming to inform Ms. Boynton that she was named as the beneficiary in a million-dollar life insurance policy on Helga Lund, but that the company was going to investigate that claim before paying it out. We're not at all comfortable with the ruling on that death."

"And neither am I," Sanchez said.

Charlotte said nothing, dreading the added motive this gave Brenda if it could be proved she knew about the policy.

"But the Frazier death compounds the issue," Sapir continued.

"How so?" Sanchez was very, very interested now.

"We also have a million-dollar policy on Bruce Frazier. And Ms. Boynton is the beneficiary on that policy also."

"Fascinating," Sanchez said. And Charlotte, whose first reaction was "oh, shit," could almost see the detective rubbing his hands in glee.

"Who took out that policy?"

"We're not sure. The name turned out to be a fake—but the premiums were paid on time. The policy is only a few months old, though. The policy is good as long as the one taking it out didn't murder Frazier. We would have discovered the fake name, of course, and investigated no matter how Frazier died. There are multiple reasons this would have been flagged before payment, but, as I saw the paperwork on both policies, I already was thinking it was a little odd and worthy of investigation. I wish to formally let the police know I'm investigating. And I really should inform Ms. Boynton directly now too. Is she available?"

"Of course she is," Sanchez said with a big smile. "She's in her dressing room. I'll take you down there; I'd very much like to see how she reacts when you tell her."

Charlotte already felt miserable about it and stood as the other two did and was ready to follow them to the door. At the door, Sanchez told a detective that he was going down to talk with Brenda again and that the detective should get the others on the set lined up for interview sessions when that was over.

"Can't do, Luis," the detective said. "You didn't tell us or them they were being detained, and they've all cleared out. Already. Except for the Trice guy. We told him he could leave, but he just smiled and said he was having too much fun—that you said he could stay."

"Shit," Sanchez exclaimed. Then he turned and apologized to Sapir for his curse, but she took it well. Charlotte got the impression Rita Sapir was well past being upset by profanity. "Well, get them all on the horn and set them up for interviews down at HQ tomorrow. What about Brandon?"

"Oh, she's still in her dressing room. You did put a guard on her, and she hasn't made a peep or shown herself outside her room."

When they got to Brenda's dressing room, though, they found out why she hadn't made a peep. Brenda was laid out on the floor in a pool of blood from a head wound.

Tony Trice, who had been waiting around down on the set for further developments, ran to the room as soon as he heard the voices of distress from Sanchez and Charlotte and brushed past them and knelt on the floor and took Brenda up in his arms.

"She's still breathing," he exclaimed, no longer giving anyone a mischievous smile. "For god's sake, someone call an ambulance."

Sanchez looked confused, Sapir looked like she was calculating all of the angles of the situation, and Charlotte, after assuring herself that Brenda wasn't dead, was looking around—and finding—a second door into the dressing room. She went to it and opened the door, to find that the makeup department was just beyond.

"I'd also put out an APB on Gretchen Lund, if I were you," she said to Sanchez in a rather trembly voice.

54

Chapter Six

"Who told you that?" David Runion demanded in a blustery voice. "I'll bet it was that vindictive bitch, Julie Javetts. And I'll bet she said nothing about her drug habit, did she? Or Aaron Woolridge, perhaps—who has been cooking the books on his productions and siphoning off money for decades."

"Please, Mr. Runion. Just calm down, please. This is a homicide investigation. We're not fishing for charges to be made on anything coming out of a blackmail scheme involving Helga Lund and Ruby Robey. We're just looking for confirmation of the activity and trying to find out how extensive it was."

Runion calmed down just a bit. It was early the next morning and they were in Woolridge's office on the set of the movie again, Sanchez having been convinced he could question the cast and crew on site as well as in police headquarters. This was Hollywood and when the show couldn't go on, production got more expensive and moguls made telephone calls. The production staff was at work on the set, but none of the principal actors and director or producer were working. All of the ones who hadn't been interviewed by Sanchez yet were lined up on chairs outside of the office and giving each other suspicious, nervous looks. Charlotte was there—but only because they wouldn't let her in to see Brenda in her hospital room until later in the afternoon.

"Is it true you were being blackmailed?"

A begrudged, "Yes."

"And that you have paid your blackmailer nearly $200,000 over the past year and a half?"

"Yes, I guess so. One loses count after a while."

"And do you know who your blackmailer was?"

"Yes, of course. They were quite open about it. Ruby Robey and Helga Lund."

"And that's all? You didn't know or suspect anyone else was involved?"

"No, just those two bitches."

"No hint that Brenda Brandon was involved?"

"No, of course not," Runion said, looking up sharply. "Brenda's a saint. I don't know what she saw in Helga, but then she has always seen the best in everyone. I never for a minute connected her with this business. How is she, by the way? Will she be all right?"

"Yes, she'll be out of the hospital in a day or two, almost as good as new. She took a blow to the back of the head, and head wounds can bleed so that the wound seems far worse than it is. She'll be back on the set in a couple of days, I'm sure. And if you put a bonnet on her, the wound won't even show for the filming."

"I was thinking of Brenda, not the film," Runion answered, with more than a touch of fire in his voice. Charlotte felt like hugging him at that point. "I hope you have found who did that to her. Was it Gretchen Lund?"

"We're working on that. Yes, you may leave now . . ." Sanchez was responding to Runion having already stood up from the chair he'd been sitting in. ". . . but I do have one more question. Who was it who suggested doing this film and asking Brenda Brandon to come back to Hollywood to play in it?"

"I don't know. I don't remember anyone mentioning that to me at all. You should ask the director or producer about that, I would think."

"Thank you, I will."

The interview with the actress Julie Javetts was even more trying than the one with David Runion.

"Oh, lord no, they weren't digging into me about drugs," she said after nearly fifteen minutes of belligerent stonewalling. "Who told you that? Wait, don't bother. Anyone out there would be happy to do so." But when she did open up, everything spilled out at a fast clip in angry words. "Who in Hollywood doesn't do drugs? No, they found that I have a sad condition. I compulsively shoplift. So far it's been nothing big and nothing that can't be smoothed over—and I'm in therapy for it. But it also isn't something I necessarily wanted to read about in Ruby Robey's gossip column. I'm on the cusp of breaking through to lead actress—especially if Brenda Brandon will just stay on the East Coast. And shoplifting is so tawdry. If I were going to be pilloried in the press, it would be so much more career enhancing that it be something mysterious and dangerous—like Brenda being considered a murderess." She simpered a sly smile at Charlotte, and Charlotte did what she could to control herself and not lean over and slap the woman silly.

"Is it true you have paid them a couple of thousands of dollars?"

"What? Yes, the sums seem laughable, don't they? A paltry amount of hush money for a silly failing. Hardly a reason to kill either Ruby or Helga, don't you think? More like scratch their eyes out."

"And would you include Brenda Brandon in that?"

"Brenda? No . . . well, not for what Ruby and Helga were up to, no. I never imagined her to be involved in any of this. She just too goody, goody. I rather hoped she was being blackmailed too. Like maybe by Helga for sex. I never could

57

quite see that pair otherwise, and it amused me to think that Helga had Brenda belled."

Charlotte's eyebrows went up when Howard Holton was brought in and nearly the only thing Detective Sanchez showed interest in asking him was where the idea for the movie had come from.

"The inspiration for the movie—and for getting Brenda back? I'd like to say it was mine. And I probably would say that," Holton said with a nervous smile, "If this were a cocktail party. But as this is a police investigation and you're taking notes, I have to say that Aaron Woolridge came to me with the idea."

Similarly, when Aaron Woolridge was brought in, this same line of questioning dominated.

"Well, John Lu had this script written for a couple of years—and he's really been plugging it. He treats his scripts like they are his children—really gets into them and lives them." Woolridge stopped there and both Sanchez and Charlotte were holding very still. For the first time this morning Charlotte felt like she was getting her bearings on what Sanchez was up to. They just waited Woolridge out as he ran through his thoughts.

"But I can say I wasn't all that keen on the idea until he came to me recently again with project, adding the idea to bring Brenda back and put her in the cameo role as the first queen. That seemed brilliant—and rather unlike John, I think. He originally had been saying Julie could be cast as the first queen and Brenda as the second. Brenda had done just that one evil role before, which I guess is what had me on the fence about filming this script. But then John suggested a switch in actresses and it all fell brilliantly in place. It will be such a shock to the public that this film will be on their lips for months—that the Brenda character is removed so early in the film."

"John Lu brought the idea to you? You're sure about that?"

"Yes. I'm sure."

"I understand that both the actors and production crew for this movie were largely an ensemble that have worked on movies together before. Is that so?"

"Yes. Mostly. The core ensemble have worked together for virtually decades—that is the male and female leads and the director and producer. Tony Trice was added belatedly at the behest of Brenda. And Julie . . . well, who knows how Julie gets into anything, but she somehow manages to do so. Of course some production people turn over fairly frequently, but Aaron and I and the principal actors have worked closely together on a good many earlier films. Not DeeDee Yance, of course. She's an ingénue being brought in to add promotional strength to this film. We often do that too."

"And John Lu. The scriptwriter. Is he part of the ensemble?"

"Yes, of course. I forgot John. He's been around since the beginning. But he's sort of like wallpaper. He's there but hardly noticeable, if you know what I mean. But I'm not really being snobby about that, I don't think. It's always seemed a trait that John cultivated. A rather secretive man that."

"And the film you made before Helga Lund died—*Woman Scorned*, I think it was called. Where she died as a character in the film died. Was John Lu the scriptwriter on that too?"

"Yes."

"Fine, thank you. That's all for now, I think. You may go, Mr. Woolridge."

Aaron Woolridge lingered there, looking confused and flushed, and he even started to murmur, "You don't want to ask me about . . . ?" But then he just let that die away, completely flummoxed. Those interviewed earlier had told him about the questions on blackmail, and he naturally assumed that would be what he'd have to talk to them about.

Like Howard Holton before him, he left the interview room in a cold sweat and wondering what miracle had saved him from revealing his innermost dirty secrets to the authorities.

Charlotte wanted to speak to Sanchez, to ask him the questions that had risen to the front of her mind over the course of the interviews. She admired his skill now, the way he honed in on the essential issues. But before she could speak, there was a knock on the door and it opened to one of Sanchez's detectives.

"Luis, we finally tracked down the Lund woman and have her here, if you want to talk with her."

"Yes, bring her in, please."

The Gretchen Lund the detective brought in didn't look a bit like the Gretchen Lund Charlotte had seen in the Hotel Bel-Air restaurant mere days before. She looked bedraggled and defeated and the light had gone out of eyes that had been filled with fire and hate before. She, however, was still as sullen as she'd been before.

"Miss Lund," Sanchez said in a booming voice that made Gretchen start and look up into his face almost as if she were coming alive for the first time in days.

Sanchez waited until Gretchen had focused on him. "I think you have been a very foolish and impetuous young woman. I understand your grief at the deaths of your mother and boyfriend, but I believe you have taken matters into your own hands, have you not? You attacked Brenda Brandon in her dressing room yesterday afternoon, did you not?"

Gretchen Lund reacted to the sternly spoken accusation as if it had been a physical body blow. She shuddered and became animated. "If you'd done your job in the first place, justice would have been done months ago and my Bruce wouldn't be dead now. She's a killer, and you've let her go free just because she's a box office star."

"No," Sanchez said in a calm voice. "Brenda Brandon is still free because she didn't murder anyone. You have attacked an innocent woman, and I'm afraid you are going to go to prison because you can't control your emotions and actions—and assume as fact what you don't know as fact and what, in fact, is not true."

"What?" The question rang out in duet. It wasn't just Gretchen who was struck between the eyes with this bold, bald statement by the detective. Charlotte had exclaimed too.

"I don't believe—" This time it was only Gretchen Lund who spoke.

"It doesn't matter if you believe me or not," the detective said. "Investigation has led to that conclusion, and someone else other than Brenda Brandon is going to be indicted for these murders—all three of them."

Gretchen continued to look disbelieving, but she didn't respond.

"Before I have the detective take you down to the station for booking and arraignment, though, I wish to have a couple of more answers from you. And you might as well answer truthfully, because whatever you say isn't going to change either your case or that of Brenda Brandon. Now, you knew about your mother's blackmail arrangement with Ruby Robey, didn't you?"

"I suspected, yes," Gretchen answered begrudgingly. "I guess I really knew, but she always denied it. I just saw too many signs of it."

"And are you charging that Brenda Brandon was also involved in those schemes?"

Gretchen took a long moment to answer, and when she did, it was almost as if a knife was slicing into her as the admission came out of her. "No, not that. Not that. I saw no evidence of that."

"Thank you for answering that truthfully," Sanchez said. And then when he spoke again, what he said didn't have quite the hard edge to it as before. "And so you knew that your mother had large sums of money in her possession?"

"Yes, I knew that."

"But do you have any proof—any evidence—that Brenda Brandon knew that?"

"No." Less reluctant than her last admission, but still not something she was happy admitting.

"Good. Thank you. I think this may not go as badly for you as it might have if you had lied to me. I think there is some leniency to be given you, considering the pressure you were under and the unfortunate circumstances. We'll have to see if Ms. Brandon wants to press charges. If not, it may not go so badly with you. So, you might give a thought or two to just how bitter you should be toward her. You have wronged her without justification. The detective will take you to police headquarters now—and I'll be along shortly to speak to the DA about what can be done—after I've had a word with Ms. Brandon."

Gretchen looked withered and cowed as she was escorted from the room.

"When did you know it was all John Lu's doing?" Charlotte asked in a quiet voice when the door shut behind Gretchen.

"Ah, you figured that out, did you?" Sanchez said as he turned his face to Charlotte.

"It became increasingly obvious as the interviews went on," Charlotte said. "Incidentally you are very good at it," she added.

Sanchez smiled, clearly pleased at the compliment from the famous FBI investigator.

"As soon as you were convinced of the breadth and depth of the blackmail scheme, you moved away from that with those you were interviewing," Charlotte continued. "And when no one—including those who might want to think so—would implicate Brenda as a coconspirator in the blackmail scheme, you moved away from that too. And you moved to the murderer's plan. You could see that Brenda was the one in danger all the time—that John Lu murdered both Helga Lund and Ruby Robey to get out from underneath a blackmail scheme that endangered him in greater magnitude than it endangered anyone else in this film community."

"True. Very good," Sanchez said.

"So, you wanted to assure yourself that it was John Lu who devised a plan to get Brenda back here, considering her a loose end he couldn't risk—thinking there was a good possibility that she at least knew of Helga and Ruby's scheme if, indeed she wasn't part of it. She lived with Helga. There was every reason for him to fear they shared their secrets."

"Right again."

"And then when Woolridge said that Lu almost lived his scripts, you pieced that together with Helga dying right out of the script of *Woman Scorned*. Added to that, the death set up for Brenda was taken from the script of this movie being shot—both scripts of John Lu. looking at the sum of those, you were home free."

"Bingo. We'll never know, of course, whether Bruce Frazier's death was a mistake or whether he was also targeted by Lu because of what he almost blurted out on the set in your presence—but it hardly matters in the end. We have him on the rest."

"But that's what I don't understand. Yesterday you still seemed so sure Brenda was your murderer. And from the start of the interviews today, you seemed to be homing in on John Lu. It's almost as if you already knew."

"I did already know. I just didn't have it all pinned down. John Lu has been slowly owning up to it all under FBI interrogation since last night. Santos Caballero telephoned me early this morning. Lu hadn't admitted to everything, although he might have done so by now. Unfortunately, chances are very good that he'll be going back to China in an exchange and we'll never see him here to face the murder charges. For that reason, if no other, I wanted to crack this case from this end myself. I didn't want to wait for him to admit to it all. It was a matter of personal pride."

"I understand. But what about the insurance policy taken out on Bruce Frazier?"

"I think that's a thread the FBI will have tied up. I think Lu will admit he took out the policy—to continually throw suspicion on Brenda so that, even in death, she would be considered guilty and he'd be free of any further investigation."

"If Santos called you this morning, though, you could have said something to me before beginning the investigation."

"Yes, I could have. But again, I needed to arrive at these conclusions myself. You haven't exactly been an objective investigative help in this. Whenever I got close to Brenda, you were throwing some obstacle in my way. You may have thought I didn't notice that you stopped Tony Trice from implicating her in anything yesterday by urging him to shut up and get an attorney, but I knew what you were up to."

"Sorry, but you're right. And I don't apologize for it. I'm retired. I don't have an obligation to be objective anymore. I believe in Brenda—and that belief is unshakable. And, I believe, it's been borne out."

"I can see your point," Sanchez said. "I wish I had someone who believed in me the way you believe in her."

"Watching the expert way you investigate, I'm rather sure you do," Charlotte answered, as she stood up and reached for her coat. It was almost time that she would be able to visit Brenda in the hospital. She was overjoyed that she would be bringing good news.

* * * *

"You had me scared there. Don't ever put yourself in danger like that again, Brenda Boynton."

"Ah, it's good to hear my real name again," Brenda said, wincing as she pushed herself up to a sitting position in her hospital bed. "It reminds me where I'm going to rush right back to as soon as I finish this film."

"So, you're going to go through with it? The filming?"

"Yes, of course. It was a commitment I made. It's not Howard's or Aaron's faults everything turned out this way. And as it turned out, it's taken a big load off my shoulders."

"And almost your head off your shoulders too," Charlotte retorted with a snort.

She didn't have long for this chit chat, though. She'd seen the car draw up to the front of the hospital as she was entering the elevator to come to Brenda's floor, and she'd stopped to talk to the detective still stationed outside Brenda's door—he not yet having been told that Brenda was neither suspect nor endangered witness anymore—and asked him to detain the man coming to Brenda's room for fifteen minutes before letting him in.

"I didn't ask for the bop on the head."

"In a way you did."

"What do you mean?"

"All the way back during the investigation of Helga's death, all you had to do was tell Detective Sanchez where you were that night—why there was so much time between when you left the studio and when you called 911 upon finding Helga's body suspended from the chandelier."

"We don't really have to get into that now, Char, do we? It's all over without that coming under discussion again, isn't it?"

"Yes, it is. But if we don't put it to rest, it will always be some secret acting as a barrier between us. And, I think, needlessly so. I think I know what your secret is, and I'm sure it will be nothing that keeps us apart in the way of not sharing it would keep us apart."

"You know? What do you think you know? How could you know?"

"It's pretty obvious to anyone who actually looks, Brenda. Tony Trice is your son, isn't he?"

There was a moment of silence, while Brenda looked away from Charlotte. When she looked back, there were tears in her eyes. "How could you have known that?"

"Just looking at the two of you, I knew," Charlotte said. "Maybe no one looks as closely as I do—sees you as deeply as I do—although that's hard to imagine. But you and Tony have the same eyes, the same smile. The family resemblance is striking. When I heard Tony drop the comment about being from Maryland, just as you are, how could I not be sure? There were multiple reasons your father whisked you away from Maryland when you were a teenager, wasn't there?"

Brenda lowered her eyes and played with the edge of a sheet with trembling slender, elegant fingers.

"What I think is that you didn't provide an alibi because you had a meeting with Tony that he didn't show up to and then when you returned to the house Helga was dead. And there must have been some reason that you thought Tony had killed her. After that you had a secret son to protect. Is that the gist of it?"

Brenda looked back at Charlotte. "Not quite, but close enough."

"Have I guessed enough for you to erase this secret between us? There is, of course, now no need to include the police in this."

"Yes, Tony is my son. I had him out of wedlock. My father was a very proud and forceful man. And my mother had just died when I found out I was pregnant. My father kept me secluded until I delivered, at which time he had an adoption set up. I was too weak in spirit to struggle with him on this. He eventually sent me here to the West Coast, and I soon was taken up with Hollywood. If I'd stayed in Maryland and tried to keep my baby, my father would still have forced a separation. But I found out where Tony had been placed and I kept up with his development. When he got old enough and showed promise as an actor, I made sure that he got out here and got a special break—all without revealing myself to him or his adoptive family."

"And the father?" Charlotte asked in a quiet voice.

"Some things are best left a secret, Char. Let's just say that he wasn't able to stand up to my father any better than I did—and that he's completely out of the picture and has been since that time."

"I can understand all of that," Charlotte said. "As much as I've seen of the world, I can understand that. But about Helga's murder?"

"It wasn't that we had a meeting planned. When I arrived home, he was there, outside the house, waiting for me. He was agitated and telling me that there was something I needed to know about Helga—and that I needed to leave her. He said he could kill her for something she was doing. He was a wild man. I coaxed him into going down to the pier on the beach with me and we talked for over an hour. He was calmer when we were done—and he didn't say anything really about why he'd said what he did about Helga. When we came up to the house, he left in his car and I discovered Helga's body."

"And you naturally thought he'd been leaving the house after killing her when you arrived. And you felt you had to protect him. Because he was your son."

"Yes. But he doesn't know. He mustn't ever know. And it's fine now, isn't it? He didn't kill Helga. It was all just a misunderstanding on my part. We can just let it drop now, can't we?"

"I think he knows, Brenda. I think he's probably known for some time. He probably knew when he came to try to make you leave Helga. The night she died."

"What? How? What makes you say that?"

"Why do you think he wanted to warn you off Helga to begin with? And you have no idea how hard he worked in the police interview to lead Detective Sanchez away from you. You also weren't conscious when we found you, so you

67

didn't see how panicked he was when we came into the room—how he embraced you and cried out for medical help. No, Brenda, I'm quite sure he knows. And I saw him arriving right after me here at the hospital today. I assume he's just outside the door. I wouldn't be surprised if he let you know that he knows today. I thought I owed it to you to prepare you for that, though."

Brenda was crying.

"We can wait until you've been able to compose yourself. But, Brenda, trust me, if he doesn't tell you, I think this is the perfect moment for you to tell him."

Within moments, Brenda was composed and looking her usual regal self, and Charlotte kissed her and backed to the door. Sure enough, Tony Trice, was just on the other side, impatiently telling the detective he wasn't a threat to Brenda and needed to see her.

When he saw Charlotte coming out of the room, he flashed that brilliant smile of his.

"It's OK if I—?" he started to say.

But Charlotte cut him off and said, "I don't think there's anyone in the world that Brenda would like to see more than you at the moment. You have your mother's blue eyes and dazzling smile, you know."

Trice first looked perplexed and then shocked, and then he was all smiles again and moving past Charlotte and into Brenda's room.

Charlotte sat outside the door, knowing that Brenda would want her to return when she and Tony had had their visit. The policeman standing guard had already been called and told that he was no longer needed to guard the hospital room door.

That's where Charlotte was when her cell phone buzzed. She looked at the caller ID and almost didn't take the call. Then curiosity got the best of her and she thought, what the hell, and picked up the phone. There were moments over the next week that she regretted she had answered it.

"Hello, Sydney," Charlotte said in guarded tones. She had been speaking to her ex-husband in guarded tones for years.

"You have to drive over here, Charley. I need you. In the worst way."

She almost clicked him off right there and then. Sydney's needs had always been in the worst way. And Charley was what he'd always called her—at first to irritate her, which it did, and years later because he either forgot it irritated her or he didn't care. She assumed the "forgot" option now, as the whine in his voice clearly defined that he needed something from her.

"Over where, Sydney?" Although it sounded OK, Charlotte couldn't pronounce his name without seeing the weird way he spelled it—like the city rather than Sidney. She wondered if his parents had done that to him on purpose, realizing from the beginning that one day he would be the brunt of everyone's jokes.

"Ocean City, Charley. The casino. I need you. I'm in big trouble."

"I'm in California, Sydney. Hollywood. I'm not at the river cottage. I can't just drive over. Besides, I thought we settled that you no longer needed me. I thought that was what changing me for Delores was all about."

"Don't be like that, Charley. They've got their thumbs on me good, and I need you. Can you take the next flight east?"

"Who's 'they'?"

"The Jersey mafia."

"I told you the Atlantic City casinos wouldn't like you opening in Ocean City, Maryland. Didn't I tell you that? Frequently? Right before you opened a casino in Ocean City."

"Yeah, you did. But the casino's doing great other than these thugs breathing down my necks. They say they're going to kill me, Charley. And they may already have killed her. I've got to raise a big chunk of cash."

"I'm retired, Sydney. I can give you some names in the Maryland state and local police and make a few calls for you, but I'm sorta busy out here."

"There isn't anybody like you for fixing things fast, Charley. And they say I've only got five days to meet their demands. Then they'll chop her and come after me. We need to raise some money, Charley."

"Chop who, Sydney?"

"Delores. Didn't I say that? They've snatched Delores and the local cops say I have to wait a couple of days even to report her missing. And that'll be too late. They've kidnapped Delores and they're going kill her—unless we can raise the cash."

Charlotte had never blamed Delores, really. Charlotte's marriage to Sydney had all been over long before there was a Delores, if truth be told. She rather pitied Delores. Delores had wound up with the booby prize— Sydney.

"OK, I'm on my way, Sydney. I've just got to wrap up something here first and I'll see about getting on the next flight."

Charlotte took a moment to compose herself and then called the airport and managed to book a seat on a plane in four hours. Then she sat there, waiting for Tony to leave Brenda's room, trying to figure out how to tell the woman she loved, who was stretched out on a hospital bed, that she had to fly away from her to try to save the bimbo who had married her ex-husband. And then she thought that Brenda was probably the one person in the world who would understand and tell her to get on a plane. That's only one reason Charlotte would never let her go.

Chapter Seven

Most of the way across country on a flight that she was wedged between a man and a woman, each of whom was almost as big as she was, to the discomfort of all three, Charlotte remonstrated with herself for becoming embroiled in her ex-husband's affairs again. She must have been in love with him once upon a time, but for the life of her, she couldn't remember when. And when she thought about it now, she realized she had married him on the rebound from a real love affair that had dead-ended. Sydney Morrison hadn't been mean to her. He just hadn't been much of anything to her for years—and although he had come from money and had held down some good jobs, he had performed mediocrely in all and had lost money in any of them that he had invested in. He also occasionally skittered on the edge of the unethical to the point of almost falling in with the illegal. Charlotte never was too sure of his moral compass. This contrasted with Charlotte, whose career in the FBI had always been on an upward spiral and one of scrupulous integrity. And as her jobs became more responsible and senior, they also became more consuming and exhausting.

For the last ten years of their marriage, the two occupied the same house but not the same space—and certainly not the same interests or dreams and aspirations. So, when Charlotte found that Sydney was being unfaithful to her, it came almost more as a relief than an outrage. And if she was surprised, it was more that Sydney had passion inside him for anything anymore. She didn't blame Delores, his former secretary and his present wife for any of this. Delores wasn't the woman who he was cheating Charlotte on when they separated—just the one with the dubious honor of being named as the "other woman" in the divorce suit. She felt sorry for Delores; she'd wound up with Sydney. And maybe that's why she was flying back across the country to see what she could do to help Sydney out of his predicament with the Atlantic City mob—a predicament she had told him he'd find himself in. She was doing it because Delores had been kidnapped in the process and Delores didn't deserve this— not on top of having to be married to Sydney.

Sydney had wanted to open a casino in Ocean City before he and Charlotte had separated; he had wanted to do it from the day Maryland had changed its gambling laws to begin to compete with New Jersey for the East Coast beach trade. But Charlotte had advised against it. Not only would it hurt her position as the senior investigator in the Maryland office of the FBI, but no one else was rushing to open a casino in Ocean City. Charlotte knew it was because of the fear of how the mob-controlled casinos in Atlantic City would react. So, Charlotte had counseled Sydney to at least wait until two or three other casinos had successfully opened. But Sydney had wanted to be the first. And he applied for his license the day after their divorce went through and had the casino going in a converted boardwalk hotel less than a year later. And so here they were.

She had left Los Angeles in mid afternoon, but since she was flying into the night by heading east, it was late night when she arrived in Baltimore. She felt groggy and wilted from how closely they had been packed into the airplane for such a great distance. By the time she was out of the luggage area and had taken a shuttle out to the remote lots to pick up her Ford Escape Hybrid, there was no way, she decided, that she'd go all the way to Ocean City tonight. It would be a 140-

mile drive. Her own town of Hopewell on the Choptank was only half that distance and just off the Highway 50 route she'd have to take to Ocean City. Charlotte had bought the Escape on a whim shortly after her divorce had gone through—attracted by its name and the symbolism of how she felt about the end of her life as Sydney's wife. But it had served her well—certainly better than Sydney had.

Stopping in Hopewell was a mistake, though. Once there, she checked on her own cottage, which was up for sale. That was no problem. But after visiting her dogs, the Siberian husky, Sam, and the boxer, Rocket, Charlotte didn't want to go anywhere. She was home now. She wanted to stay here and wait for Brenda to come home and then hide from the world with her. The dogs were being taken care of quite well, of course. While Charlotte and Brenda were in California, they were being kept by Charlotte's school-teacher friend, Sherry Landon, who was renting the house next door to Charlotte's cottage. The folks who owned the house Sherry was renting were the real owners of Sam, but they had been off on archeological digs for so long that Charlotte had supplanted them in Sam's life.

Reluctantly, she said good-bye to the dogs again and drove back up River Street to Brenda's house. After Helga's death, Brenda had escaped Hollywood and come back to her childhood home—and to the house the prominent Boyntons had occupied for centuries. Her house was a federal-style manse, the original plantation house for the area that eventually was developed as the town—more a village—of Hopewell. And after Charlotte and Brenda had found each other, Brenda had convinced Charlotte to sell her own house farther up the street, which paralleled the Choptank River. So, Brenda's house was now Charlotte's house too—and that's where she went now to spend the night.

As tired as she was, she didn't consciously notice the black Lincoln sedan with two men in it sitting at the curb across the street from Brenda's house in front of the Joyce and Todd Vale's Hopewell B&B.

* * * *

"A black sedan with two men in it," was the first thought Charlotte had the next morning when she woke up. It wasn't that she hadn't seen the car the previous night or that it hadn't struck her as odd to see two men sitting in a car on a quiet village street late at night. And it wasn't that her investigator instincts had let that slide. She had just been too tired from the cross-country flight and all of the stress she'd been under with the suspicion thrown on Brenda back in L.A. to have been operating on all cylinders the previous night.

She struggled up out of bed and padded out to the hallway and to one of the front bedrooms. She and Brenda shared the master bedroom at the back of the house. Looking out the window, she could see that there still was a dark sedan sitting in front of the Vales' B&B across the road. She couldn't be sure that it was the same sedan she'd seen the previous night. She didn't see anyone sitting in the sedan now. She scanned the front of the inn. Maybe there was someone at one of the windows, but maybe not. With the shadowing, it was too difficult to tell—and Charlotte knew that wishful thinking might put someone there in her mind who wasn't really there in fact.

She picked up the telephone and dialed the inn, and Joyce Vale, who wasn't particularly a friend of Charlotte's since Charlotte's sleuthing had led to the incarceration of Joyce's daughter earlier in the year, answered. Charlotte had hoped for Todd, who wasn't the young woman's father and hadn't done much to play sides in that issue.

"I thought you were tagging along behind Brenda Boynton in Hollywood," Joyce said when Charlotte identified herself.

"I came home early but am off again this morning for some business in Ocean City. But I noticed two men sitting in a car that was parked out in front of your inn late last night. And I noticed the same car might still be there. I'm just checking to see if you folks are all right."

"We're just fine, Charlotte. Thanks for asking." Joyce's tone didn't sound all that thankful. And she certainly didn't sound like she was in the mood to chat.

"Then you have two men staying at the—?"

"Sorry, we don't gossip about our guests. And they have separate rooms, if that's what you're asking."

"Thanks, Joyce. But that, of course, wasn't what I was going to ask. Hope you and Todd have a lovely day." Then she clicked off before Joyce had the pleasure of doing so.

Her cell phone was ringing almost as soon as she'd hung the house phone up, and her first thought was that it was Joyce calling back with another jab or two. But it was worse than that.

"Sorry to be calling in the middle of the night. But can we meet today—as soon as possible? It's important."

Charlotte recognized the voice of the Santos Caballero, chief agent of the FBI in Los Angeles.

"Sorry, Santos. I can't. I flew back to the East Coast yesterday. Something's come up here."

"Well, I guess that's a good thing then. I wanted to let you know that John Lu managed to escape as he was being transferred to the L.A. jail awaiting arraignment. And he may be gunning for you. We didn't mislead him on who had connected the dots on his spy and murder activities."

"OK, I'll keep that in my mind. Did he escape early or late yesterday?"

"Late. Why do you ask?"

"No particular reason. I just wondered how long he'd been on the loose." What she really wondered was whether he had time to get to the East Coast before she did and park out in front of her house—or to get any of his East Coast

75

contacts to do so. "Let me know when you've caught him again," Charlotte said.

"Will do. Take care now."

"Same to you."

She caught a quick breakfast from whatever she could find in the pantry—they'd let their perishables deplete before taking off for the West Coast—packed enough fresh clothes for a week, and went into the garage through the kitchen door at the back of the house. She briefly looked longingly at Brenda's distinctively vintage Jaguar XK-E sports convertible as something that would impress Sydney. But then she reminded herself that she had no need or desire to impress Sydney and certainly had a great need to conserve the cost of gas. So she climbed into her Ford Escape and backed it out of the garage.

She backed far enough out into the street to be positioned to where she could read and record the license plate number of the dark sedan parked across the street. It had a New York tag on it. She copied the number down in her gas log book and started out to catch Route 50 above Cambridge where it crossed the mouth of the Choptank.

She hadn't gotten any farther west toward Ocean City on Route 50 than the small town of Linkwood when she realized that the dark Lincoln sedan was on her tail. Once again there were two male occupants. Dark hair, surly aspects, and both rather bulky looking.

Charlotte took her cell phone out of her purse and clicked in a number. She'd never do this on the move if she didn't have to keep on the move. She couldn't very well stop at the side of the road to do anything about two guys tailing her, though; she'd be setting herself up for an easy assault. As she fiddled with the cell phone, she wondered how anyone actually was able to use one and drive at the same time.

Luckily David Burch was on the other end after the first ring. Burch was a county deputy sheriff—and very likely going to move up in the next election—who was not only the most eligible bachelor for miles around but also knew Charlotte well and had used her investigative skills in his own work.

"David, this is Charlotte Diamond. I'm just back from California and on Highway 50 in Linkwood, headed for Ocean City."

"Got a problem I can help with?"

"Yes, please. I'm being tailed by two men in a black Lincoln, who were parked in front of the Vales' B&B last night and possibly casing Brenda's house, or waiting for me. I've been told there's a fugitive in a spy and murder case who may be gunning for me, although there's no evidence connecting these two. Anything you can do in getting them off my tail?"

"Sure thing. Stay at the speed limit unless they try to overtake you. I'll send the nearest cruiser over to you and get out there myself before you get too much farther. And keep your cell phone line accessible until I'm there. You got a license number I can check?"

"Yes, I do," she said and gave it to him. Then she worked on trying to keep herself from hyperventilating until she saw a police car gliding in behind the black sedan. Soon there were two, and as the parade of four cars entered Salisbury, the black sedan turned north on Route 13, as Charlotte continued on 50, just as if that had been what it was going to do all along.

Twenty minutes later, Charlotte's cell phone rang. It was Burch. This time she pulled over to the shoulder of the highway to take the call.

"You know guys named Furnari or Spera? Or the car owner, someone named Joseph Crea from Jersey City? He's got a small fleet of these cars."

"No, I've never heard of any of them. Did you get anything out of them?"

"Claimed they were just driving from Baltimore back to New York and taking the scenic route. Stayed in Hopewell,

Furnari said, because his sister recommended the B&B there. Want me to call the Vales and do some checking?"

"No thanks. I doubt they'd be helpful. And I suppose the men claimed not to know me or to have been tailing me."

"Got that right. Should I do more checking?"

"No, thanks, Dave. This might be connected with an FBI case, so I think I can get them to do some checking. Thanks loads for helping me out, though."

"Any time you need us, Charlotte. Any time."

Charlotte stopped one more time to use the cell phone before having to make the decision whether to stay on Route 50 proper and hit the beach at its south end or take the Ocean City Expressway and cross onto the barrier island at Ocean City's midpoint.

"Been waiting for you to show, Charlotte," Sydney answered when she managed to get through to him via the casino switchboard. "I'm in panic here."

"I couldn't have made it last night, Sydney. But I need you to tell me where the casino is. I'm on 50 east of Salisbury. Should I stay on 50 or should I take the expressway?"

"The Expressway. Turn north on the Coastal Highway when you've hit the beach. The casino's at the north end of Asawoman Bay at the corner of Jamestown Road. Have you rattled the cops and made them interested in finding Dolores yet?"

"I'm waiting until I see what's what, Sydney. Be there in a bit."

"That's just as well. I know that if we can just get them the money they demand, this will all work out well. I don't really want to start a war with the Jersey mob."

Shortly after she pulled back onto the highway, she thought she might have seen the black Lincoln back on her tail, but at a more discrete distance behind her. But she wasn't so sure that she made any effort to do anything about it. She was in a steady stream of traffic now. If they hadn't done anything when she was on a more deserted stretch of road, she had to believe they were just keeping tabs on her, not setting up to take any sort of action.

For the umpteenth time since Sydney had called her in Los Angeles yesterday, Charlotte wondered why in the hell she was sinking into any sort of involvement in Sydney's problems at all. She had looked forward to Sydney getting all of his problems in the divorce settlement to work out on his own.

Chapter Eight

"Five hundred thousand dollars? No, I don't have that kind of money, Sydney. We were married for two decades. Where did you think I'd scraped together money like that? I'm here to see what I can do to help you with Delores's kidnapping, but if you called on me in hopes I'd have the ransom money, you're out of luck."

"I'm sure Brenda Brandon is loaded," he said.

He sat there, in a lounge elevated four steps over the casino floor in Ocean City's Ocean Front Hotel and Casino, looking cool as a cucumber—certainly more calm than any distraught husband whose wife had been kidnapped by mobsters that Charlotte had ever seen—and got right to the point of hitting her up for a half a million dollars—because of who Charlotte had gone to after he and she had split.

Charlotte did what she could to restrain herself from reaching across the table and slugging him one. Before that she had been giving him points on what he'd done with the casino. She had been quite surprised when she drove up to the front entrance of the casino—a semicircular, three-lane drive with a gaggle of car hops waiting under a canopy extending across all three lanes who were ready to hand her a tag and whisk her Escape away.

Sydney had been standing there at the entrance waiting for her. And she had to admit that he looked very good too. He was wearing a well-tailored three-piece suit and was tall and distinguished looking. That was the one thing he'd always done well in their marriage—he had dressed well and looked very good on her arm. He had escorted Charlotte to the myriad of luncheons and charity balls that a senior FBI official was expected to attend and had drawn the admiration of all of the women. He stood straight and hadn't put on weight and his face was tanned and relaxed—as a result, Charlotte knew, of spending more time on the tennis court or golf course than in his office doing business.

She had expected him to look frazzled and worn down. Not just because of Delores's predicament but because of the weight of actually having to juggle all of the work involved in managing something like a casino and hotel. But he didn't look frazzled; he looked like he was in his element. This was Charlotte's first clue on how indispensable Delores must be to this operation.

And when Charlotte had gotten inside the main casino hall, she was impressed with the efficiency and sparkling clean and plush interior here too. The casino certainly wasn't as big and luxurious as those in Las Vegas, but it was in excellent condition, was laid out well, and was being enjoyed by a large number of patrons.

"It looks great," she couldn't help but muttering.

"Mostly Delores's doing. She's always seemed to know just how everything should be set up and how the flow should work. We've done well from the beginning."

"I'm sure, but—" Charlotte hadn't completed the sentence. She'd always done everything just right herself, she thought. And Sydney had always managed to screw up everything she'd done. What was Delores's secret, she wondered. But she didn't say anything. She hadn't come here to fight with Sydney.

Sydney waited until they were seated in the lounge and had ordered drinks before he made his pitch for ransom money.

"I don't know what else I can do, Charley. I'm at the end of my rope on this. The police just stonewalled me."

"Let's start from the beginning, shall we? When did Delores disappear and how do you know she was kidnapped . . . and what is needed for ransom?"

"You don't believe me, do you?" Sydney gave Charlotte a glare, and she did a double take in shock. It had never occurred to her not to believe him. Ah, what the passage of time can do, she thought. There was a time when she would not have been so quick to believe him.

"I just want to have it all laid out in order, Sydney. That's how we solve cases."

"I just want Delores back. I don't need to have the Atlantic City mob even more mad at me. Can you bring them down, Charley? If not, can we just get Delores back?"

"We can start that by you telling me everything about her disappearance, Sydney."

Sydney told Charlotte how Delores hadn't come up from the gaming floor the night before the previous one.

"You live in the hotel?"

"Yes, we have an apartment in the penthouse."

And then he told Charlotte how he'd gone to sleep before Delores came up to the apartment—and when he woke, she wasn't there. There was just an envelope under the door with a note in it saying that he had just five days to come up with half a million in cash for Delores's release or he could deed 10 percent of the casino to a Atlantic City casino, the Black Flacon. It was really a piece of his casino that they wanted, Sydney was sure.

"That's unusual," Charlotte said. "They've given us a way to trace them down. We can work on following the paperwork to whoever wants the slice of the casino."

"I just want Delores back, Charley. We just need to think of a way to pay the ransom."

"We can start by finding out who owns the Black Falcon."

"I know who owns the Black Falcon. It's the Vario mobster family. And if we go to them on this, we'll all have our throats slit."

"Vario? Paolo Vario?"

"See, even you know of them. And you'll know that this is all too big for us. We just need to get the money."

"You said you went to the police. Did the note tell you not to? And I'll need to see the note, by the way."

"It disappeared."

"The note disappeared?"

"Yes. I read it and laid it somewhere and then I couldn't find it. They have someone on the inside here, Charley, watching me—probably watching us at this very minute. That's why we just need to . . ." Charlotte was waving what he wanted to say off, so Sydney went on to the other questions. "Yes, I went to the police. I don't remember what the note said about the police. But it was a waste of time. The police here are as corrupt as they get. I wouldn't be surprised to hear they were in Paulo Vario's pocket. I went to them and they did nothing. They said it was too soon, but I didn't get the impression they ever would care. We don't have time for the police, Charley. Let's just forget about them."

"Who did you talk to in the police department?"

"Who did I talk to?" Sydney looked confused and his face went blank. "I don't know. They weren't offering any help. Somebody by the name of Dixon, or something like that. Maybe his first name was Frank. I don't know. I just know I was beside myself and they weren't being any help. We don't have time for—"

"OK, OK, we do have some time. I'll see what I can do. I'll call the FBI office in Annapolis. It looks like racketeering. And if she was kidnapped to New Jersey, that would have been across state lines and that should be at least good enough for me to start with the FBI."

"Thanks, Charley. So, maybe the FBI will swing for the ransom?"

"We'll see, Sydney. For now, though, I need to find someplace to stay and make some phone calls."

"You can stay here. We have plenty of vacant rooms. I'll set you up."

As Sydney walked away and Charlotte searched through her purse for her cell phone, she got the sinking feeling that Sydney was going to be a pain in the ass during this entire ordeal. And then she laughed bitterly at the thought that she'd have half a million dollars to turn over to save the life of the woman who had replaced her in his bed. Just like Sidney to try to gouge Brenda through her. Of course, if she did have the money she would be willing to do it if it saved Delores's life. Dollars to donuts, though, Delores was already dead. Charlotte had been in the business long enough to know the circumstances were either not good—or very fishy. Maybe both.

* * * *

The room Charlotte was given at the casino was quite plush. It was on the fifth floor with a full expanse of window and a balcony overlooking the ocean. The furniture looked like it was several steps above the usual motel fare, and she could have been convinced that the tiling in the commodious bathroom was real marble. This business must be pretty lucrative, she thought.

She didn't unpack but went straight to the balcony and stood looking over the ocean for a long moment. The running of the waves onto shore was mesmerizing, and she was momentarily far, far away—with Brenda—looking out on the Pacific. It struck her for the first time that she'd been on the West Coast for several days, overlooking a different ocean from a hotel terrace and she'd never gone down to the California beach. She decided not to make the same mistake here. When she'd been with the FBI, she'd often come to the shore when she had a particularly vexing and elusive problem facing her. And she'd just walk the beach and watch the water lapping up on the shore. This usually helped her mind focus on the issue she was trying to resolve.

"Usually" was the operable word. Sometimes it didn't help a bit and she had to work out her problem another way. Otherwise she'd just run to the beach each time she was embroiled in a conundrum and that would be that.

She'd try the beach routine here, though—after she made a phone call.

She went back into the room and called a former assistant of hers at the Annapolis FBI office, Margaret Fancel. Margaret was now Charlotte's quickest link into the FBI world.

"Yes, I'm personally fine, Margaret," Charlotte said. Margaret had picked up on the first ring and had shown delight that Charlotte called. "Yes, I had a good trip to the West coast."

"And you can't escape your past, I hear," Margaret said down the line. "I hope you're keeping your head down. The last I heard they hadn't caught up with Edward Chang. But it's such a relief to have that case closed now. You're doing great work for us even in retirement."

"Ah, you heard about the apprehension of Edward Chang—who we found to be the Hollywood scriptwriter John Lu—then. That was a lucky find. He just dropped into my lap. I'm afraid I'm calling about some more possible FBI work—an across-state-lines kidnapping and also possible racketeering. And I'm sorry to say there's some personal involvement, so I hope I can get some help without raising screams of favoritism."

"Anything for you, Charlotte. Although I may be overstepping a bit. We have a new chief agent here, and he's a real stickler. But tell me what you have and need and I'll see if wheels can be set in motion."

Charlotte proceeded to give Margaret the background on Delores's and Sydney's predicament, and she threw in the names David Burch had given her of the men who followed her from Hopewell and of the owner of the car they were driving.

"That's quite a tale and a tall order, Charlotte. I'll see what I can do, but I might not be able to get back to you until the morning."

"I'm completely at your mercy and beholden to you for anything you can do, Margaret. I'll keep my cell phone with me and have it on. I'll check with the police down here, but I'd like to know what I can about their reputation and who this detective is who might be named Frank Dixon before I start over there. As the ex-wife, I'd probably be seen more as a good suspect by them than a collaborator."

"We can make introductions for you down there, if it would help."

"Let's keep that option open until you've found out whatever you can on my questions. But, thanks for the offer. And good luck with that bear of a new boss you say you have there in Annapolis."

When she rang off, Charlotte changed into something scruffy and went down to the boardwalk and started walking the beach and thinking. She became conscious that she was checking the face of every tall, slim man she passed for Oriental features. Even though she'd shoved John Lu to the back of her mind, her instincts had her on the alert that he might pop up unexpectedly—and unpleasantly. When this thought surfaced, Charlotte realized she hadn't brought the handgun with her that she'd picked up at home during her overnight stop en route to the beach from the airport. But she never had liked carrying that and had avoided doing so as much as possible.

The walk helped clear her mind, and when she returned to the casino, she started tracking down the employees who had been on duty the night that Delores had disappeared.

"She works late," the house manager for that night said. "She's everywhere, observing everything in the evening hours. As often as not, she can be found roaming the casino floor."

"Did you see her that night?"

"Up to about 2:00 AM, yes. She checks with the cashiers every two hours or so and, if they've taken in a large amount of cash, she strips the excess off the top and puts it in the safe. I was there at 2:00 when she stopped by."

"Was there excess cash?"

"Yes."

"And where's the safe?"

"It's in the basement. It's one of those big bank vaults. It's a real rats' warren down there, but the vault was so heavy the Morrisons had it installed on the concrete slab down there."

"Did you see any suspicious men or women paying particular attention to Delores?"

"Suspicious men and women in a casino at night? You must be joking." Both laughed. "But, no, I didn't notice anyone paying particularly close attention to Mrs. Morrison—other than the usual looks the men patrons give her. She strikes quite a figure in the tight dresses she wears in here."

Without thinking, Charlotte sucked in her stomach—and cursed all slim blondes under her breath—as she parted with the house manager and walked away.

A hatcheck girl helped Charlotte determine that Delores most likely was snatched in the basement while making that run to the vault.

"Yes, I remember her going downstairs," the young woman said. "From my station, I have a clear view of the door to the basement stairs, and I remember her going down—because she was with a man. And, no, I don't remember her coming back up. But when I get busy, I don't notice what's going on down the corridor anyway. She might have returned. But I didn't see her for the rest of the night that I can remember."

"Do you remember anything about the man she was with or if Mrs. Morrison seemed distressed?"

"He was just a man in a dark blue suit. Hefty, sort of meaty looking. But nothing special for the casino. And if she was distressed about anything, it wasn't anything that I noticed."

Charlotte thanked her and went down to the basement. It was a real labyrinth of rooms, just as described. But most of it was taken up with a parking garage that extended down a couple of more stories. Charlotte walked around the rooms that were in the part that wasn't parking garage. She found the office where the vault was located. The door to the office was locked, but there was a window in the door. She tried in her mind to account for all of the space down there, but it was cut up too haphazardly to do so. What she did know was that there was a clear shot into the parking garage and, once there, anyone could have bundled Delores into a waiting car and taken off.

She went out into the garage, finding that the door from the corridor she was in opened into the garage close and at an angle to the attendant's booth by the car entrance.

Charlotte walked up to the booth. The guy sitting there with ear plugs from a portable radio stuck in his ears, a gangly younger guy with a scraggly goatee, watched her warily as she approached him.

"Can you tell me who was on duty here two nights ago—the night shift, at about 2:00 AM?"

"You a cop or somethin', lady?"

"No. I was something once, but not now. But call Mr. Morrison or your supervisor, please, and ask them if you can respond to questions from Charlotte Diamond. And if you get your supervisor, maybe ask him the same question about who was on duty here at 2:00 AM that night."

Still looking at her like she was going to mug him, the attendant lifted and dialed the phone. He was put in order soon, though, and when he handed the telephone over to Charlotte, the supervisor had tracked down the man who was on duty the night Delores disappeared and patched him through to where she could talk to him on the phone.

"Yes, ma'am, I know who Mrs. Morrison is and would recognize her if I saw her. No, I didn't see her in the garage that night. Not at 2:00 AM or anytime. But it's possible she came through and I missed her. I had to contend with a couple of drunks who decided to park in the exit about that time."

"Thanks," Charlotte said. "Any cars backed up by that episode?"

"Nah, not really. It was pretty dead in the garage. That time of night, most of the gamblers park in the surface lot. I guess they can't wait to get into the slots and tables."

Determined now more than before, Charlotte went into the basement area and searched what she could, although several of the doors were locked. She made a mental note to pull Sydney down here with keys and do a better search. When she went back up in the casino, though, she couldn't locate Sydney and decided that the search could wait. She was too weary to continue tonight and it didn't help that Sydney didn't seem all that interested either. She went to the elevator.

Back in her room, Charlotte showered and stretched out on the bed and made an hour-long telephone call to Brenda, hearing that Brenda was fine and out of the hospital and almost finished with her cameo role. Charlotte then unburdened everything she had been doing and what was transpiring with the problem here in Ocean City. She knew she was whining too much about Sydney and of his problems as being an albatross around her neck, but Brenda was a good listener—and she was perhaps the only person in the world that Charlotte could be entirely open with like this. After they spoke and had said good-bye for the eighth time, Charlotte clicked the phone and the bed lights off and started drifting off to sleep.

Her dreams were of wandering around in the rabbit warren of rooms underneath the casino, with the sound of raucous laughter and the spinning of roulette wheels reaching down to her in the catacombs from the gaming room above—and looking for something without the slightest notion what she was looking for.

Chapter Nine

"Oh, good, you're there. I almost gave up on you. I do have much of the information you wanted, Charlotte, but there's a rub."

Charlotte had slept so soundly that she hadn't heard her alarm. She had no idea she was this tired. She chalked it up to jet lag and the aftereffects of adrenaline pumping. She did hear the cell phone tone, though, and reached for it after the third ring. She knocked it off the nightstand, searched around under the edge of the bed for it, and came up with the instrument on its fifth ring.

"A rub?"

"Yes. You can have the information, I'm told. But you have to come here to get it."

"Go there? To Annapolis from Ocean City?"

"Yes, I'm afraid so. The new boss wants you to come to him personally to get it. He can be in the office late this afternoon, if you can make it."

"I guess I'll have to," Charlotte said, with a groan. "At this rate, I'd save time by hiring a water taxi. I've never made this many trips around the whole length of the Chesapeake Bay in this short of a time before."

"And, Charlotte. This is the weird part. He says you will need to block out the evening too and wear a ball gown."

"A ball gown? What kind of jokester is this new boss of yours?"

"Normally the serious, insistent type. He said I couldn't tell you any more than that. But he also said he had some information you would want to know. He doubts that the situation is as it seems."

"I've doubted that too. OK, but better make it 4:00 PM or later. I've now got to stop in Hopewell again. I didn't bring any evening wear with me to the beach."

"Not a Boy Scout, then? You didn't go to the beach fully prepared?"

"Apparently not," Charlotte answered.

"Well, there's no reason you should drive all this way in formal dress. I'll meet you at my apartment. You can change there. And you're welcome to spend the night there too."

"Thanks, Margaret, you're a lifesaver."

When Charlotte clicked off the phone, she looked around the room as if she'd never been there before. Then she muttered an "oh, shit," under her breath and picked up the house phone to order a breakfast. She wasn't even sure she owned any evening wear that would fit her anymore.

* * * *

"You tick out really, really well, Charlotte Diamond."

He couldn't have possibly known about her mad dash through a department store for a new dress or the quick stab a hairdresser made at her unruly hair in the limited time she'd had to travel and make herself presentable. So, he was on her good side from the beginning.

"Evan? Evan Worthington? *You* are the new chief agent in Maryland for the FBI?"

"Yes, that's me. What were you expecting? Come let me look at you." He stood up from his desk, towering over Charlotte, who was no midget herself. He'd put on some weight—perhaps a tad more than was fully necessary—but Charlotte couldn't fault him on that, as she'd done so as well.

But he was the same ruggedly handsome man she had been wooed by—and, yes, bedded by—back in the early days in Quantico and then had lost to Ruth Singletary.

They stood there, facing each other in his commodious office, hands held in hands, and looking each other up and down—and neither one being particularly disappointed in what they'd seen.

"Well, you aren't quite the ogre I'd expected."

"Oh, is that how the staff here see me already?" Worthington asked. "I thought it would take me at least a couple of months to clue them in to that."

"No, it isn't what I was told. But the summons and the dress code. I thought I was being brought to the principal's office for a dressing down and having my hand slapped for trying to bring the FBI in on my personal problems."

"Ah, commanding a dressing up so that I could apply a dressing down. That's good. I'll have to remember that one for later, when I feel like torturing the crew."

"You always were able to make me laugh," Charlotte said after having done so. "But seriously, why the evening dress? And let me take the opportunity to tell you in all honesty that you look very presentable in that tux."

"I have a tailor who can make a walrus look trim," Worthington said. "Come, sit down over here. Business first. Then I'll take you out to Les Folies Brasserie for dinner—I'd prefer Cantler's Riverside Inn, and the staff tells me that is a favorite of yours—but we might stand out like penguins in the tropics if we go there in these getups. And later we're going to the governor's mansion. I had no trouble getting you added to the guest list. He said he had something to talk to you about anyway."

"The governor has something to talk to me about?" Charlotte said. She already was breathless and this bit of information wasn't helping. "I'm sorry, could you slow down? I haven't gotten beyond finding you sitting behind this desk. The last I knew you were doing the circuit of embassies in Europe in liaison positions. Weren't you working with Interpol in Paris?"

"Yes, I was. But there came a point in time when I needed a radical change. I came back to Washington for a couple of years and then, when I felt fully up to it, they assigned me here. You don't know how disappointed I was to find that you had retired before I got here. I'll have to admit that one reason for accepting this assignment was you."

"Me?" Charlotte asked. She had managed to slide into a chair facing Worthington's desk while he moved to his position behind it. Just having this much of a separation from him was clearing her head. He had been the love of her life and she had taken it hard when Ruth had slipped between them. Charlotte and Evan had had a spat—a serious one— and on the rebound Ruth had taken advantage of his vulnerability and Charlotte's absence. He had married Ruth because she told him she was pregnant. But there was no issue from her claim, and they had started their life together in a state of mistrust. Charlotte had accepted the first assignment away from Quantico that she could. In the intervening years, she'd heard that Ruth and Evan's marriage was a bit rocky, but Charlotte had maintained her distance and had married the first man who asked her. Sydney had been a spoiled Philadelphia mainliner, but he'd been spiffy on the surface, and Charlotte hadn't bothered—or, perhaps, dared—to look below the surface for nearly two decades. Her loss, of course.

"You wanted to work with me?"

"That too. More to the point, I wanted to be with you."

Charlotte felt herself trembling and she looked away so that Evan couldn't look into her eyes. She had no idea what he would see there and how he would interpret what he saw. But she somehow knew that she had to guard against him seeing anything. This wasn't Quantico of twenty years ago. She had found her true self now—and she had found it with Brenda. Nothing would shake that. She tried telling herself that, even as she already was feeling that she was shaken to her very foundation.

She cleared her throat and looked up, looking for something that would take them off this tack, but what she found pulled her even farther into the abyss. "You said you requested a transfer from the international division."

"Yes. Ruth died. Cancer. It lasted several years and brought us closer together—and then tore us apart. After she died, I needed a complete change in environment and some time to heal."

Charlotte said nothing. She was holding her breath, having no idea what to say.

"And, as I said, I'm sorry you weren't still on the roster when I got here. But I understand you're just on the other side of the bay. A place called Hopewell on the Choptank, isn't it?"

"Yes. And it's a very restful place. I needed a complete change too."

"But I understand that you haven't been able to rest—that you've landed yourself in a couple of mysteries you've had to unravel. That business with Win Eagleton was a real hot potato. And now you've come to us with yet another can of worms."

Charlotte steamed into the opening he was providing, consciously shutting all of those doors of vulnerability he had opened. "Yes, what I came to your office for. I was told you had some answers you could give me for the questions I asked—and maybe some help with the problem."

"Answers, yes. Help, I'm not so sure. We're willing to give you any assistance we can, of course. But we couldn't really find a handle on any of this that would spell FBI interest."

"Oh, I'm sorry to hear that. Please tell me what you found out."

"It's more what we didn't find out, I'm afraid. First, the only Frank Dixon—or any name similar to that—in the Ocean City police department works vice way down in West Ocean City. And there was no record of anyone reporting a Delores Morrison as being abducted. You asked about Paolo Vario, who your ex-husband said might be involved. He's a racketeer all right, and we'd be very interested in pursuing anything he was involved in. But he's based in New York and, to our knowledge—and we do have informants in his organization and we did check this out yesterday evening—he has no interest in the Atlantic City gambling scene at all. You'd mentioned the Black Falcon. He doesn't own that. He works Las Vegas on anything connected with casinos. One of our informants laughed at us and said Atlantic City was too small time for Vario and then couldn't stop laughing when we mentioned Ocean City.

"We checked out those three names you gave us regarding your being followed into Ocean City. Joseph Crea owns a couple of the smaller Atlantic City casinos and Toto Furnari and Carmine Spera are both goons of his. He's the one who owns the Black Falcon. I'm concerned you were followed by them. I've asked the office in New Jersey to squeeze them on that, and I'll let you know what turns up. At least Crea will then know you are still one of ours and that we care. And that's usually enough for us to tell a small-time operator like Crea."

"Thanks, Evan. I'll have to think about that. The Ocean City police might just be stonewalling, though. Sydney told me they showed no interest. Do you have any indication that there may be corruption there? They might be part of a shakedown operation themselves."

"We've thought of that and are checking it out. Resort city police departments have rather a bad reputation for that sort of thing—I would think a city trying to become a gambling center would have more problems than most with police corruption. But one other thing, Charlotte."

"What?"

"I'm concerned about this John Lu who is running free somewhere. I read the case file on that and it has your name stamped all over it. This is a big case. And I'm worried about you. I don't know what this business is with Joseph Crea, but we're not ruling out that it may have something to do with John Lu. I'd . . . we'd like you to be very careful until we can put Lu away again. And I'll let you know if we find any connection with Crea."

"Thanks again, Evan. Just one more favor, please. Could you run these two names through your files to see what sort of background you can come up with?"

Charlotte had written two names on a note pad she'd seen on Worthington's desk. She tore off the top sheet and handed it to him. He raised his eyebrows when he saw it and seemed surprised. "This is exactly why we're all sorry you're still not here with us, Charlotte. We hadn't even thought of checking into these two. But, of course, it's right that we do so—if you don't mind?"

"Of course I mind. But it has to be done."

Worthington turned on his charm over a candlelight dinner. Charlotte felt like she was being wooed again as he'd done down in Virginia when she'd first been swept off her feet and coaxed into his bed. He was surfacing conflicting emotions in her. But he was a master. He would hone in just to the right degree and then back off. And, as she always had been, she became lost in his good humor. Her sides—already crushed by the girdle she'd had to tighten to be able to fit into any of the evening gowns she'd found in the department store—were aching when they finally arrived at the governor's mansion.

The two of them immediately got lost in a sea of socialites, minor celebrities, the obligatory bureaucrats—which both Evan and Charlotte realized was their category—and political contributors basking in the privilege of bending and knocking elbows in the governor's mansion.

They weren't so lost in the crowd, however, that Charlotte wasn't sought out by the one of the governor's staffers and asked to attend him in the library. There, the atmosphere of being among the angels and powerful was much more rarified than out in the entertainment rooms.

Governor O'Malley was standing at the Victorian-era mantle of the library of the house dating back to the mid-nineteenth century and was receiving people, individually or in small groups, who were being brought to him. He wasn't speaking to anyone very long, and between visitations he was turning to his chief of staff, who stood to his right and slightly behind him, presumably to check out what he had to say or request of the next person brought to him.

Charlotte was befuddled when she was asked to step forward, but Worthington was following right behind her, which she found to be both a blessing and a threat. She couldn't become involved with this man again. She kept pounding that thought into her brain. She was a different person now. Her world was just perfect now. Or so she had thought before Evan Worthington dropped back into her life. And right at the moment she found it quite comforting to have him at her side.

"Ms. Diamond, it's such a pleasure to meet you again. I'd ask how you were enjoying retirement down on the Choptank, but the news over that last year and more indicates you are still busy solving mysteries."

Charlotte was nonplused. She had no idea the governor would even know who she was—even though they had met fleetingly from time to time before she had retired and before he'd become governor, when he was the state's attorney general. And she certainly didn't know he'd have any idea where she now lived or what she did there. But she just assumed he was being fed that information by his chief of staff. It was a bit comforting—and just a bit frightening too—to see that the Maryland government was in the hands of such a well-oiled machine.

"Thank you, but I really am trying to not be noticed any more at all."

"Well, we can't really have that," the governor said, with a laugh. He looked over her shoulder at Worthington and said, "Can we, Evan? I think the FBI really should coax her back into service. I know I, for one, would sleep better at night."

"And I also—with her back in bed with us," Worthington said. He was smirking more than smiling, Charlotte thought, and she felt herself blushing under the foundation of makeup she'd applied to try to hide the age spots on her cheeks.

"What I'd like to see, Ms. Diamond—and why I was happy to learn that Evan was bringing you here tonight—is for you to continue to serve us in Maryland in some capacity."

"I . . . I don't know how I could help," Charlotte responded. "I really have looked forward to retirement."

"Yes, I see how you've adjusted to retirement, Ms. Diamond," the governor answered, with a laugh. "You seem to be more in the news with your sleuthing now than when you worked for the bureau."

And then when Charlotte couldn't find anything pithy to answer to that, he continued. "What we have in mind is membership on one of our state commissions. I was thinking of the Gambling Commission. It's just forming in response to our new gambling laws. It would be the natural place to use your talents, I would think."

"But that, of course, would be quite impossible," Charlotte answered.

"Oh, how so?" the governor answered. He looked sharply at her, and she could see a flash of pique. Obviously the governor wasn't accustomed to disagreement.

"Wouldn't that be a gross conflict of interest? My ex-husband, Sydney Morrison, owes one of the new casinos in

Ocean City. That would make it quite impossible for me to serve on the Gambling Commission."

"Your ex-husband? Owns an Ocean City casino?"

"Yes, the Ocean Front Hotel and Casino—at the corner of the Coastal Highway and Jamestown Road."

"Owns a casino? I didn't know that." The governor seemed flustered and turned to his chief of staff, who looked equally flustered and whispered to his boss in a voice clearly heard by both Charlotte and Evan, "Nothing like that came up in the background check. I'll have that checked right away."

"Well, if not that commission, certainly another one, I hope. We'll be back in touch with you. I do hope you'll take on service in some capacity, though." He was still rattled.

"I would be happy to consider the possibilities," Charlotte answered politely, doing what she could not to make an awkward situation even more so. She could see the chief of staff starting to sweat and the governor fighting his frown as she was led away to be replaced with the next victim on the governor's list. Or this was the way Charlotte viewed the audience—as a victim.

As they walked away, Worthington muttered, "I see that we have some more checking to do ourselves."

Yes, Charlotte thought, either the governor's administration wasn't nearly as well oiled as she'd thought, or Sydney had been playing her for a fool.

It wasn't more than a few minutes after that that Charlotte became tired of this governor's reception event and suggested that they leave.

"Fine with me," Worthington said. "But you don't really want to go all of the way back to either Ocean City or Hopewell tonight, do you? I need to stop back by the office, but then perhaps you'd like to come to my place. There's plenty of room, and—"

"Thank you, no, Evan. It's been a memorable afternoon and evening, but just take me back to the office

100

with you. I've already arranged to spend the night with Margaret Fancel. She'll be happy to meet us there and take me off your hands."

"I don't know that I want anyone to take you off my hands," Worthington said in a low, melodious voice. "Can't we—?"

"I don't know, Evan. It's all going too fast now. I've moved on. But I just don't know. Please don't press. We can talk again . . . sometime."

He retreated than, and, as he probably knew, Charlotte was even more attracted to him than before because he wasn't pressing her. She almost regretted that he hadn't pressed her when Margaret met her in front of the FBI Annapolis bureau and whisked her away. But almost immediately Charlotte's thoughts went to two things—the ever-more muddied waters of the Delores kidnapping case—and the need to get to a phone in private and call Brenda and hear her reassuring voice once more.

Charlotte tried calling Brenda before retiring at Margaret's Annapolis apartment overlooking Deep Creek, but she was shunted off to voice mail.

She stopped in Hopewell again on her way back to Ocean City and played with the dogs for a while and dusted in the house, knowing that Brenda should be returning home any day. She also checked with the realty company to see how the sale of her own cottage up River Road was going. There had been nibbles, but the market was bad, and the realtor suggested that Charlotte just hang on if she didn't need the money from the sale soon.

"You have waterfront. Don't sell it short."

"OK," Charlotte answered. "But it would be nice to sell it soon."

"Have you thought of keeping it for rental? It would make a great vacation property. And . . . and you never can tell when you might need or want to move into it again."

Although she agreed to consider turning it into a rental—and acknowledged that this might be the wisest thing to do—she had considered her willingness to give it all up and have only Brenda's place to call home a symbol of her commitment to their relationship. When the Realtor had suggested undoubtedly the wiser move, Charlotte's thoughts had immediately gone to Evan Worthington. And the guilt had flooded in. Never before in the past several months had she suffered a second thought about her relationship with Brenda.

"Damn Evan for showing up again," she muttered.

"What was that?" the Realtor asked.

"Oh, nothing. Yes, yes, I will consider making it a rental if it doesn't sell soon. Let's discuss it again in another week or so."

By the time Charlotte got on the road again, it was getting dark—and she had a two-hour drive ahead of her. Her mind was racing on all sorts of things. It would have gone on overload if she'd parked her car in the garage, however. If she'd done so, she would have noticed that Brenda's Jaguar roadster was missing.

* * * *

"Hello, Charlotte. We were wondering when you'd get back."

The surprise that Charlotte had felt when she drove into the parking lot of the Ocean City casino to find it jammed with cars overflowing from the garage below and having to leave the Escape at the mercy of the car hops who were really hopping turned into shock as she walked into the casino and saw Delores Morrison. The supposedly absent woman was decked out in a tight red sheath evening gown and gliding around the casino floor in dangly earrings, jangly bracelets, a trim figure that set Charlotte's teeth on edge, and perky little breasts. She was slithering down the aisles and smiling here, giving a little frown there, the queen of the casino—and so cool and collected you'd never had thought she had been gone for three days, let alone held prisoner with her life threatened.

The whole casino seemed surreal. The car lot full, but there didn't seem to be any more patrons at the slots or on the tables than the last evening Charlotte had been there. So, where was everyone?

Charlotte gave a little hysterical laugh, though. Why was she worrying about a discrepancy in cars and people, when she was standing there looking at a woman who she thought was being held for ransom—and who appeared more calm and collected than she was? Delores saw Charlotte standing in the foyer as it opened into the games floor, though, and waved regally and then sauntered over to her.

"But you're supposed to be—"

"Oh, that was just a little misunderstanding. I was spending a couple of nights with a girlfriend up at Fenwick Island, and I thought I'd left a note for Sydney. But he said he hadn't found one. No big deal."

"No big deal, Delores? Sydney said he'd gotten a ransom note and had gone to the police—and I was with the FBI all day yesterday. Not a big—?"

Delores put her hands on Charlotte's arm and started guiding her down the elevated path running alongside the gaming floor. "Come into the theater. I've got something I think you'll want to see. Did Sydney show you the theater? We usually only have talent on the weekend and we keep the room closed the other days. But there's something special in there tonight. It's been the talk of the town all afternoon. We're really packing them in."

And "packing them in" was right. As Charlotte reached the entrance into the theater, she saw that it was standing room only in there and now she knew where all of the people from the jammed parking lot were.

Her jaw dropped to her chest when she looked up on the stage to find all of the lights spotted on the black-silk-clad chanteuse standing at the center mike and singing a sultry song in a dusky alto that had every eye and ear in the place trained on her, straining to take it in.

I had no idea Brenda Boynton was a singer, was Charlotte's first thought—when she was able to unfreeze her brain and have a thought.

Chapter Ten

"You never told me you could sing like that."

"And dance too. There's so much you still have to learn about me." Brenda was smiling smoothly as Charlotte guided her, hand on arm and none too delicately, into the lounge overlooking the gaming room and plopped her down in a barrel chair. "Most of those in the movies came up through stage work where they had to do it all."

"But what are you doing here?"

"Singing. And protecting my investment."

"Your investment? Explain, please. You didn't tell me you were flying back East this soon."

"I didn't know it myself until late last night, which was early morning your time—and you have your cell phone switched off."

Charlotte dove into her purse for her cell phone. "So I do," she said. When she turned it on, she saw that there were messages waiting for her in addition to the ones Brenda had sent. No time for that now, though. "What do you mean your investment? And why are you here—performing? Did you do it just to surprise and please me?"

"Hmmm. I hadn't thought of doing it for that reason. Would it have worked?"

"Yes, probably, if you had done it for that reason, but you've now pretty much shot that as an excuse."

"And what would have been my reward for surprising and pleasing you?"

"Knock it off, Brenda. Why are you here?"

"I'm a part owner in this casino now. And I thought you'd be here—that this was where you'd be, waiting for me."

Charlotte blanched at the not having been here—especially considering where she'd been and who she'd been with instead. But Brenda didn't pick up the tension in the air. She continued with her explanation.

"When I got here, I decided that, while I waited for you—wherever you were; meeting a mysterious handsome man, no doubt—I might as well make myself useful. As a part owner. And the expression on your face when you came into the theater was priceless."

Charlotte had a strong twinge of feelings of guilt over the reference to a handsome man, but she shoved those aside. "A part owner? What have you done, Brenda?"

"Among other things, I helped set Delores Morrison free. That's what you wanted, isn't it? To get her free so you could pull back out of contact with your ex-husband. Or did I read you incorrectly from your phone call the other night? You said Sydney needed a half a million to clean this up, and I have much more than that sitting around doing nothing—and two million coming from California when the insurance company acknowledges that there is no reason now why I shouldn't get paid out on the insurance policies taken out on Helga and Bruce Frazier. They were legally taken out in my name, and I'm not in any way responsible for their deaths. And there's the money I'm inheriting from Helga's estate—although I'm still willing to let Gretchen have all of that."

"Oh, Brenda. I didn't mean for you to do anything like that. You shouldn't have done that."

"I didn't think you'd be overjoyed, but I wanted you back and not concerned about your ex-husband's problems. I didn't do any work to get the money. So, can we just go back to Hopewell now and get on with our lives?"

"I love you for making the effort. But it isn't as simple as that. You don't just pay off kidnappers and waltz off into a fairy-tale ending. What percentage of the casino did Sydney give you anyway?"

"Ten percent. Even my broker thought that was a good deal. I have little interest in the casino, but it's a hotel in good condition on the beach. I've had the tour. It's top notch."

"Been to the basement too?"

"There's a basement? Well, no, but what does that—?"

"Never mind. I think I'm just being ironic."

At that moment Charlotte's cell phone started chirping and she looked at the number of the incoming call. "I've got to get this. It's from the FBI in Annapolis. They've been sending me voice mails all afternoon, and I didn't realize I had the phone turned off."

"Fine. I have another set to sing in the theater anyway. We can talk later. I've had my things moved into the room they put you in, by the way."

"Terrific," Charlotte said, but she didn't watch Brenda glide away from the table—although everyone else in the lounge had appreciative eyes turned to her—because her mind already was tuned into the call from Annapolis.

When she was finished with the call—which took considerable time, because she had revelations about Delores Morrison's reappearance to convey herself—Charlotte struggled out of her tub chair and started looking for Brenda.

But she couldn't find Brenda.

The ushers in the theater said that Brenda had never come back to sing another set. So, Charlotte, steamed, went looking for Sydney and Delores.

She didn't find them; they found her. Both of them rushed up, looking distraught. Sydney was waving a piece of paper in front of him with one hand and pulling at his hair with the other.

"They've taken Brenda Brandon now, Charlotte," he exclaimed breathlessly as he approached Charlotte. "And now they want a million dollars."

Charlotte raised her hand and backhanded Sydney across the cheek, sending him staggering back into Delores's arms. Delores's eyes went big, and she was giving Charlotte a terrified look like Charlotte had gone mad.

"Cut the crap, Sydney," Charlotte declared. "Take me to the basement—to wherever Delores was hiding out—and to where you've stashed Brenda. You better not have harmed a hair on her head, either, or I'll tear you limb from limb before the police get here. Do you hear that? Those sirens are for you and Delores—and whatever other members of the Crea clan we can roll up in this garbage of a shakedown."

So steamed was Charlotte that she made the mistake of taking off for the basement herself. By the time she reached the bottom of the stairs, Sydney and Delores were no longer with her. Charlotte was bent on finding Brenda as fast as possible and making sure she was all right. The police arrived soon thereafter and helped Charlotte in the hunt. But it was she herself ultimately who found the false door in the office with the vault in it that was made from a bookcase and that, when they broke the lock, led them into a plushly appointed apartment and an unconscious Brenda Brandon, drugged and laid out on a twin bed. These were the rooms Charlotte had been looking for earlier, knowing, intuitively, that Delores probably never had left the casino, dragged away by kidnappers.

The police had less luck catching Sydney and Delores before they made off.

"I suggest you call the police in Atlantic City and have them try the Black Falcon hotel and casino there," Charlotte told the policemen. "With luck the police can be waiting there when the two arrive."

But Sydney and Delores didn't arrive at the Black Falcon, and although Sydney was now out of Charlotte's presence again, he was in the wind and she had no idea when he would be showing up again to mess up her life.

* * * *

"If I didn't know I was hallucinating, I'd think I was stretched out in an Adirondack chair, staring at the Choptank."

"Oh, good, you seem to be completely back with us," Charlotte whispered as she bent down and gave Brenda a kiss on the forehead. "And, yes, you are on the banks of the Choptank. Thanks to David Burch, we got you and your roadster back home. I told them I thought you'd like to wake up in your own backyard. The drug they gave you was powerful, but it was relatively harmless. It was just supposed to keep you sleeping until those two scarfed up their million and beat it."

"Who's those two? And what million? And wasn't I wearing something a little more slinky than these jeans and flannel shirt the last time I was awake—and not so much like a tent." Brenda groaned and moved to her side, giving her a view toward the mouth of the Choptank into the Chesapeake. Then she sighed.

At that moment Charlotte knew she was right to bring Brenda back home before she regained consciousness—before anyone in the casino saw her slack-jawed and drooling. Charlotte had called David Burch to come help and they'd gotten her bundled straight out of the basement of the casino into a smoked-glass limousine in the garage and away from Ocean City before any reporters showed up on the scene.

"This is the Brenda I want," Charlotte said, as she lowered herself into a lawn chair beside her companion. "In grungies and completely in my power. I'm afraid you were taken for a ride and your casino-owner days are numbered. And don't worry. I did all of the clothes changing. If anyone saw you being carried out of the Ocean Front, I didn't want them to connect you with the chanteuse who had wowed them in the theater earlier in the evening. The clothes are mine. No more cracks about being able to swim in them, please."

"I wouldn't think of it. But I hope they don't fall off when I stand."

"And I hope they do," Charlotte cracked. She was happy to hear that Brenda managed a tinkly laugh at that.

"What's this about my not owning a piece of the casino? I assure you I have a receipt."

"And you also have your $500,000 back. That receipt is worthless, although we might frame it and inscribed it with the title 'Brenda's Folly' and hang it in the dining room, where it can give us both indigestion. Sydney didn't have 10 percent of anything to sell you. And the real owner of the casino isn't someone you would want to partner with. Although he's quite displeased, I'm sure, to hear that he had a claimant to a chunk of the place who he didn't know about."

"The real owner?"

"Yep. Sydney didn't have any stake in the casino. His wife may have because she was a Crea. But I'm afraid she's not one the Crea family would be happy to accept at the moment."

"A Crea?"

"Yep. I probably could have saved you the long sleep and brush with racketeers by having kept my cell phone on. The FBI was trying to reach me all day yesterday—yes, you've slept into the next day. I'd asked them to do background checks on both Delores and Sydney. It turns out Delores's maiden name is Crea. She's Joseph Crea's niece. He heads a minor mobster family with its fingers in casinos in Atlantic City. I sent the police to his Black Falcon casino, thinking Sydney and Delores might go there—but it turns out that's about the last place they'd try to escape to. The Creas weren't upset Sydney was setting up a casino in Ocean City. They own it and were using him as a front man. And the reason that Delores had such a good touch in setting the casino up and keeping it running in tip-top shape is that she had experience doing so in her family's casinos in New Jersey."

"But if they didn't need the money . . ."

"Oh Delores and Sydney needed the money all right. While you were snoozing out here, I was on the phone to the casino's accounting firm—which is pretty much controlled by the Crea syndicate in Atlantic City. It seems that good old Sydney and Delores have been skimming profits off the casino and the accounting firm was about to find that out. They needed $500,000 and fast. And so they staged Delores's kidnapping. Sydney didn't need me to find her; he needed me to find him $500,000 quick. They staged Delores's kidnapping and then kidnapped you for real, and pushed their luck."

"But I gave him the $500,000. Why did they kidnap me as well?"

"Probably because you told him you were about to come into about three million. You did tell Sydney that, didn't you?"

"Yes, I guess I did. I wanted him to know that I could easily afford what he needed to spring his wife loose. I guess I set myself up for kidnapping, didn't I?"

"That's right, honey. Right after I told you not to give me a heart attack and get yourself in danger again, you flipped right over to the other coast and landed yourself in a lobster pot."

"I was only trying to help," Brenda said plaintively.

"I know that. But I say again, 'Don't ever do that again.' As for Sydney and Delores, I stirred up a hornets' nest by siccing the FBI on the Crea operation in Atlantic City. Uncle Joseph must have figured out what Delores and Sydney were up to and then they didn't need just the $500,000 to top off the accounts—which they probably were going to do even when caught to prevent Joseph from really going after them. Now they needed getaway money. When you dropped that you had all of that cash rolling in from your California excursion, they pulled a Delores snatch scheme on you."

"But you were on to them."

"I thought something was fishy from the beginning, yes. But when that report came back giving Delores's maiden name as Crea, it all fit into place."

"They still haven't tracked down Sydney and his new wife?" And then in a more strained voice, "You don't think the New Jersey mobs have found them first, do you?"

"I've got to believe that they are still out there—they probably have at least part of the money they embezzled to help them keep on the move. I think if Sydney were dead, I'd know it."

"The easing of stress?" Brenda asked.

"I'm afraid so. But let's not talk about Sydney and his bimbo anymore."

They were silent for a while, both enjoying the breeze off the river and the start of a sunset across the water in the west.

"And what about John Lu?" Brenda asked in a low voice. "How does he fit in? And do we have to lock the windows at night?"

"Yes, Brenda, we have to lock the windows at night. How many times have I told you it's a big, bad world out there? But we shouldn't have to worry about John Lu. He had nothing to do with what was happening here. When those two goons came here to follow me, they were working on Delores's orders, not those of her Uncle Joseph. That's one of the reasons I started questioning Sydney's role in all of this. He was the only one who knew I was flying back to Maryland that day. And he probably figured—rightly—that I'd make an overnight stop in Hopewell. Delores and Sydney wanted to keep track of me and make sure I was going to show up and drop into their trap. John Lu has been caught. He was trying to board a Chinese freighter in San Diego. The

Chinese will probably get him back, but the FBI wants to squeeze him some more. He never left the West Coast."

"You know what would go well with this glorious sunset?" Brenda asked.

"Wine. But you're not having any until at least tomorrow. We want to make sure you are up to it and there are no bad aftereffects of the drugs."

"We?"

"Yes. Me and Sam and Rocket. The boys are trapped back in the house. If I let them out now, they'd be all over you. I don't want to have saved your sweet butt only to have your own dogs maul you to death. When you're strong enough to walk, we'll go back to the house, and then they can be all over you. I don't think they liked us being gone for almost two weeks. Even though Sherry spoiled them mercilessly, I can tell. We're going to have to train them all over again, I'm afraid."

"That's too bad, because I was just thinking that I'd like to get away—just the two of us. Not to do any more movies. I've had enough of that and of the West Coast for quite some time. And nothing as weird as becoming casino mobsters either. I mean a long vacation completely out of our elements."

Charlotte liked that idea. She liked it even more than she could reveal to Brenda. She was still feeling guilty and conflicted about the return of Evan Worthington to her life. To get completely away from him—and in the company of Brenda—might be just what she needed.

"I'm game. The boys don't want to admit it, but they adore Sherry. She pampers them in ways we don't. We can put off training them until we get back from wherever we vacation. Sherry can take the brunt of letting them get the upper hand."

"I've often thought about a river trip in Europe," Brenda mused, almost to herself. "Maybe down the Rhine.

The Christmas markets. New Years in Amsterdam. Something entirely different."

"That's certainly entirely different; you know that I'm the world's worst shopper. And you know how I feel about the cold."

"Oh, we wouldn't buy—and I did say someplace completely out of our element. It would be a good excuse to do a lot of cuddling. And as for the shopping, we'd just take it all in with our eyes. Something fabulous and completely different—and completely out of both of our characters."

"You certainly make it sound challenging. We'll have to give it some—"

But then Charlotte's cell phone started chirping and she looked at the caller ID. The name that floated up was Evan Worthington. Her trembling finger hovered over the answer button.

"How far away is the Rhine?" she turned and asked Brenda.

Olivia Stowe

Olivia Stowe is a published author under different names and in other dimensions of fiction and nonfiction and lives quietly in a university town with an indulgent spouse and two demanding Siamese cats.

Books By Olivia Stowe
Charlotte Diamond Mysteries
By the Howling
Retired With Prejudice
Coast to Coast

Other books
Fiddler's Rest
Spirit of Christmas
Chatham Square

www.cyberworldpublishing.com